DIRTY DESIRES

A BAD BOY BILLIONAIRE ROMANCE (DIRTY NETWORK BOOK THREE)

MICHELLE LOVE

HOT AND STEAMY ROMANCE

CONTENTS

Made in "The United States" by:

Michelle Love

© Copyright 2020

ISBN: 978-1-64808-710-3

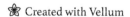 Created with Vellum

BLURB

Lost love can be hard to overcome, but maybe she can help me find my way back again ...
Her backside is what first caught my attention.
Round, firm, plump, juicy. Those are the words that ran through my mind when I first saw her bent over the table in front of me.
For a couple of years, she'd filled my fantasies, and now she was filling my dreams too.
But someone else had lived in my dreams for a long time. I didn't want her knocking that person out of my life forever.
Pushing her away seemed impossible. No matter how hard I tried, my arms kept pulling her back to me.
And just when I was able to let it all go, it all came crashing down on me again.
Had I been cursed? Doomed to live life without love? Or could she break that spell?

CHAPTER ONE

Nina

I inhaled the exquisite scent of the espresso I brewed in the Hammacher Schlemmer Four Specific Brew Barista Machine my friend and coworker Lila Cofield had bought for me to create Liquid Heaven. That's what she and my other coworker Julia Wolfe called anything I brewed up for our late morning pick-me-ups at WOLF, the news network we all worked for.

We would convene in Lila's office around ten each and every weekday to chat about anything and everything as we sipped on some high-octane formula to keep going strong throughout the day. Well, until lunch anyway.

We had worked together for a little over two years and knew each other inside and out. Julia had married the owner of the network, Artimus Wolfe, not long after she went to work as his assistant. Lila was the co-anchor of the Morning News and she and her co-anchor, Duke Cofield, had begun seeing each other not long after they started working together. After a two-year relationship, they'd gotten married just a couple of months ago.

And then there was me. Nina Kramer, cue card girl, social media assistant to Lila, and single as could be.

I had my eye on a man who also worked at our network. But with over two years passing without us becoming anything more than just friends, I had nearly lost hope of anything progressing between us.

The office door opened and Lila and Julia came in with upturned noses to take in the coffee's aroma. "Is it almost ready, Nina?" Lila looked past me, checking out the machine.

"Almost." I got the mugs ready, placing them on the table as the last bit of espresso came out. "Have a seat, and I'll serve it up shortly."

Julia and Lila took seats across from one another on the two sofas that faced each other. We had a little triangle laid out and I always sat in the chair at the pinnacle of the sofas. It made for easier group chatting that way.

The round coffee table in the middle served us all. Julia had brought blueberry scones and laid them out nicely on a paper lace doily. "I picked these up at the bakery two blocks over. I haven't tried them yet. I hope they're as yummy as they look."

Running one hand through her blonde ponytail, Lila winked at Julia. "I'm sure they're delicious, Julia. So, what's this big news you were talking about as we walked to my office? I admit, you've got me very curious."

I filled the cups with a mixture of coffee, espresso, and caramel cream, then placed them on the table in front of my friends. "Here you go, girls. And what's this news, Julia? I'm curious too."

Julia picked up the mug, taking a long sniff of the coffee before she'd even say a word. Lila and I exchanged glances, her right eyebrow raised, her blue eyes sparkling the way they always did when she was set on getting some answers. Always the journalist was our Lila.

We both turned our eyes on Julia. Her long dark hair had been pulled back; her big brown eyes seemed to laugh at us. "You two! It's nothing, really"

Lila was adamant. "You can't say you've got big news then just shut up, Julia. Come on. Spill it."

"Yeah, Julia. Spill it." I sipped my coffee as I continued to stare at her.

"Okay," she finally gave in. "Artimus and I are going to start trying for a baby."

I was stunned.

Lila was ecstatic as she jumped up and went to grab Julia up in a hug. "I'm so happy for you two!"

It wasn't that I wasn't happy for her and Artimus, but I was feeling left out.

And just as I had nearly pulled myself together to stand up and join in the hug, Lila burst out, "Me and Duke are trying too!"

"Ah!" the two of them screamed as they jumped up and down.

Now I really felt left out. I sat there in silence, trying to push the selfish thoughts out of my head, but they wouldn't be pushed away.

Why have I waited so long for Ashton Lange to realize we're meant to be together?

Now here were my best friends having babies. Or trying to, anyway.

Both of them were married, and now they were both working on growing their families with the men they loved. And what was I doing?

Making coffee, writing on cue cards, and answering tweets for Lila. And nothing else!

My social calendar seemed be too full of time spent waiting on Ashton Lange to make a move. Now I was beginning to realize just how stupid that had been on my part.

The sudden silence made me look up at my friends, only to find them looking right back at me. Julia looked back to Lila. "Maybe this wasn't the best time to say something," she said, looking a little shamefaced.

Then I was at the center of the hugs and attention. That only served to make me feel worse. "Quit it, you guys. I'm fine."

They let me go and took their seats once more. Lila patted me on the leg. "No, you're not fine. And this needs to be said, Nina. It's time to shit or get off the pot."

Julia nodded. "It is. It really is. You waiting around for Ashton doesn't seem to be working, Nina. Look, I know he's a great guy, but he's got issues that run too deep."

Taking a drink of my coffee, I knew she was right. "It does seem like he can't get over losing his fiancée. I mean it's been years now. If his grieving or guilt or whatever is going on in his head hasn't subsided by now, then I doubt it ever will."

Ashton Lange, the station's favorite producer, had been engaged once upon a time. It had been about four years since the accident that took the woman's life. Ashton had been at the wheel of the car, from what I'd been told. Not that he'd ever told me a thing. Others had.

Ashton and I were pretty close. We were great friends. I had always thought that would lead to something further someday. Two years later, I wasn't sure anymore.

Julia clucked her tongue, taking my attention away from staring into the creamy abyss inside my coffee mug. "Before you just go and decide Ashton isn't worth your time, let me ask you. What it is that attracts you to him?"

That was easy. "His demeanor. He's sweet, thoughtful, caring, perfect in every way." I put my mug down, kicked off my heels, then pulled my feet underneath me. "And he's so cute. Those blond wavy locks that fall to the tops of his shoulders—they're hard to resist running my hands through. And when he wears it in a man bun at the base of his neck, my lips ache to kiss that exposed neck, to trail my lips up and down."

Lila laughed. "Oh, honey, you've got it bad."

"She does, doesn't she?" Julia asked, then sipped her coffee. "What else attracts you to him, Nina?"

His eyes shone in my mind. "Those cerulean blue eyes dance when he's being funny. And then there's his body—tall, muscular—and his ability to be completely sexy on top of all the rest of his attributes. He's the total package. To me he is, anyway."

Julia sat up, and I could tell she'd put on her thinking cap as her dark eyes were wide and her lips were pursed. "Okay, so let's lay this all down so we can help you figure out where to start with this man who you are clearly so hopelessly in love with."

"In love?" I shook my head. "Let's not go that far. I can admit that I'm insanely attracted to Ashton, but I can't say that I'm in love with him. Not when we haven't even kissed. Or gone out on a date, I might add."

Lila wagged her finger at me. "You two eat lunch together almost every day. And sometimes dinner too. Now, in my opinion, that's a date."

"Not mine." I laid my head back on the chair as I imagined what the end of a date with Ashton would be like. "My idea of a date ends with a kiss. Not a 'See ya later, Nina,' the way our lunches and dinners always end."

Julia agreed, "I can see where she's coming from. Okay, so let me help you see things clearly here, Nina. You have wanted this man for two years now. Your only competition is the memory of his dead fiancée. He hasn't dated at all since I've known him, which is as long as I've worked here at WOLF. I think that's a good sign, don't you?"

I had to admit that it didn't hurt anything, "It's an okay sign, I guess. But that sign has been lit up for a couple of years now and so far, it hasn't helped me a bit."

Lila stood up and put her hands on her hips, looking as if she had a plan. "Okay, here's what you're going to do. You're going to put things into motion, Nina. No more waiting around. You've got to be proactive."

Julia agreed, "Yeah, be proactive, Nina." She stood up too. "Now, what would a proactive woman do when she was out to prove to the man she wanted that she was worth moving on from the memory of a lost love?"

They looked at me as if I knew the answer to that. My eyes moved back and forth, looking at each of them. "Are you two being serious? Obviously, I don't know the answer to that question or I wouldn't be here, getting stared at and lectured by two women who have every-thing else all figured out."

Lila looked at Julia and asked, "Do you think you've got it all figured out, Julia?"

She shook her head. "I know I don't. But what I did have going for me is that I knew what I wanted. I wanted Artimus. He wanted me. And we made it happen."

"I don't know if Ashton wants me." I chewed on my fingernail as I thought about that. "What if he doesn't?"

Lila scoffed at the idea. "Phooey! He wants you. We've all seen him look at you with pure lust and sometimes he just smiles when you walk by. He's into you, big time. I think he's just afraid of losing a woman he loves again. You have to let him know that he doesn't have to be afraid."

"And how can I do that?" I had no idea how to help anyone stop being afraid of anything, never mind help someone stop being afraid of death or losing loved ones. When they both shrugged, I wanted to jump up and pull their hair. "Ugh! This is impossible."

"It is not," Julia said with a stern tone.

"She's right," Lila added. "Nothing is impossible unless you allow it to be. And you're not going to allow that, Nina."

"I'm not?" I was feeling skeptical and not a little self-pitying.

Julia stomped her foot. "Heck, no, you're not going to allow that. Now let's brainstorm. What is it that wins a man over almost every time?"

Lila smiled. "Sex."

I sighed and shook my head. "I'm not going to just go to his office and offer my body up to him, Lila. So, think of something else."

Julia looked at Lila as if she were crazy. "Come on, Lila. Be for real here. We both know Nina isn't that kind of girl. She's not the type to seduce him by wearing nothing but an overcoat, before dropping it and leaving her naked body on full display for the man. She's just not the type, even if it would bring Ashton to his knees, begging to worship at her altar."

I had to laugh, because that was just ridiculous. "You guys don't know the man at all, it seems."

They both looked at me as Lila said, "But you do. Now let that sink in, and now come up with at least one thing you can do to put a chink in that armor he has around his heart."

Standing up, I decided I was going to give this a real shot. And my nose led me right to one of my secret weapons, which everyone loved. "Some women say the way to a man's heart is through his stomach."

At least I had one idea to work with.

CHAPTER TWO

Ashton

An enchanting scent wafted past my nose as I sat at my desk in my office at WOLF, reading about how lighting could be used in the studio to enhance the viewer's watching experience. The smell had me looking up to find Nina Kramer coming in with a mug of steaming coffee in her hands. "Hi there."

I pushed the papers away and leaned back in my chair, taking her all in. "Hey, Nina."

Her ash blonde hair was pulled back into a hairclip and her green eyes sparkled as she set the mug down in front of me. "I brought you something I've concocted."

It was well known that Nina brewed a mean pot of coffee. She and her friends, Lila and Julia, had powwows around ten each morning, and everyone knew that coffee took center stage.

Our boss, Artimus Wolfe, seemed to be the only man who had ever been offered a cup of the magical liquid. Being Julia's husband had its advantages, I supposed.

And here I was, the recipient of a cup of bliss, handed to me by the maker herself. "Thank you. And to what do I owe this honor?"

Nina took the seat in front of my desk, which wasn't unusual. We were good friends, and we had been since the inception of WOLF. I was the one who'd hired her as the cue card girl in the very beginning. There'd been something about her that I'd just liked right off the bat.

First of all, she was easy on the eyes. To me, she was a petite little thing. Being six feet and two inches myself, a bit on the taller side, her five-foot-five height made her seem small to me. The smattering of freckles that dusted across her nose and the tops of her cheeks made her look adorable.

But Nina had a sexy quality to her too. Round hips and a butt that wouldn't quit were offset by a tiny waist. Her tits were world-class too. At least a size D, I'd guess. But those were all things I tried very hard not to notice on a day-to-day basis.

I loved the way she dressed, too. Always so professional. And it was no different as she sat in front of me, offering me coffee. Nude heels made her legs look long and lean. A form-fitting navy blue skirt hugged her curves well, and a tan lace blouse tucked into that skirt completed the outfit perfectly. My eyes were glued to the mounds of plump flesh just underneath that fabric. I pulled them away to look her in the eyes.

Really, I tried hard not to dwell on her many attributes.

Her smile was bright as she said, "I just thought you might like to try some of my coffee is all."

Picking it up, I took a sip and found my taste buds dancing with delight. "This is great, Nina. I'd heard tell that you were once a barista —and one hell of a great one at that. But I was certain it had to be a myth. In two years of working together, I have never seen a cup of the mystical brew."

She laughed and leaned back in the chair, making herself comfortable. "And now that you have, what do you think?"

"I think I'm already addicted." I took another sip and knew I wasn't lying about the addiction; the coffee was fabulous. "I hope this isn't a tease, girl."

"Nah, I think I can bring you a mug each day." She leaned

forward to whisper, "But you can't tell a soul. I don't want to end up making pot after pot each day for everyone else. This is a special thing, and I only do it for special people."

I'm special to her?

I knew I was kind of special to her, but not coffee-special. "Lucky me." I took another sip then sighed. "It really is wonderful. Thank you."

"I was thinking a while ago that I don't know that much about you." She looked over her shoulder at the open door. "Mind if I close that, Ashton?"

I had no idea what she was on about, so I nodded. "You can close it."

She got up, closed the door, then came back to sit down. "We've worked together for a pretty long time, and yet I hardly know one personal thing about you. Like your family. Where are they?"

"My parents moved from New Jersey, where my older sister and I grew up, to Georgia." I leaned back, resting my head on my clasped hands. "Mom inherited her grandparent's small farm there. My parents sold their home and moved a few years ago. My sister, Annabelle, is married with two kids. They live in Hawaii. Her husband is the manager of a hotel there. We get together once a year at the farm on my parents' wedding anniversary. Other than that, we only talk on the phone, as everyone has their lives to lead."

"You live alone in your Manhattan apartment, don't you?" she asked, then her lips formed a straight line, and one small crease moved across her brow. It gave me the impression that she was concerned about my living arrangement for some reason.

"I do live alone. And if you know someone who is in need of a place to live, I'm not really interested. I like my life just the way it is, and I'm not into having a roommate. I like the solitude of living alone." I leaned forward to rest my elbows on the desk as I looked at her.

She shook her head. "I don't know anyone who needs a place to live. I was just asking. You see, I'm curious, Ashton. I know you were engaged once, and I know what happened. Did she live with you in that apartment and you just don't want anyone else to intrude on her memory?"

My heart stopped beating. I'd told only my closest friends, Artimus and Duke about that. I should've expected that they would tell their wives about the accident and that the wives, being Nina's best friends, would tell her. But why she was bringing it up now, I didn't understand.

Shoving my hands through my hair, I pulled it back as I thought about what to say. Finally, something came to me, "No, she and I didn't live in that apartment together. I had to move out of the place she and I shared. I couldn't stand to be there without her."

"Before her, did you have roommates? Or did you live at home with your parents?" She gave me a stoic stare, as if she were analyzing me.

I wasn't sure if I liked it or not, but my mouth kept talking anyway, "I lived in the dorm at Columbia before moving in with her."

"So, you'd always lived with other people until she passed away, and since then you've lived alone." She shook her head. "How can you stand that? I mean, I've lived with other people my whole life. I can't imagine living all alone."

I wasn't about to tell her that I would rather live alone than have anyone know that I still had nightmares about the accident that took my fiancée's life. About once a week I would wake up screaming. No one needed to hear that.

With a shrug, I said, "I like it that way, Nina."

A smile curved her plump pink lips. "How'd you meet her, Ashton? How did you meet this woman that you asked to spend the rest of your life with?"

No one had asked me that since before she died. I gazed into Nina's eyes as I told her about that time in my life. "A few friends of mine and I were on spring break in Florida. Her family owned the hotel we were staying at in Miami. Her parents had brought her from India only a few months earlier, and they all worked for her uncle there. She worked in housekeeping, and we ran out of towels. I was looking for more and was sent to the laundry room by the man at the front desk to get some there."

"Was it love at first sight?" Nina asked with wide eyes.

I laughed. "Yeah, it was." I could see her face in my mind. "She was sweaty and aggravated when I came into the laundry room and asked if I could have four towels. She didn't even turn around as she shouted at me that I would have to wait, they were still drying. Then she turned around and saw me. She and I just looked at each other for a long time in silence, and then she apologized."

Nina sighed then said, "So that's what love at first sight is. Interesting. How long did it take before you two became a couple?"

"No time at all. I ended up hanging out with her all of spring break. She wanted to go to college, so when I got back to New York, I got a job and a small apartment and then she came to live with me. We lived together for six months before I asked her to marry me. She wanted a big wedding. Her family was happy with that and was going to pay for all of it, as it was their tradition as Hindus. The date was set for a year from the day I proposed."

Nina looked a little sad as she asked, "What was her name, Ashton?"

No one had asked me that since her death. I hesitated to even say it for fear I might break down, but then I let it slip from my tongue, "Natalia Reddy. She was beautiful and fun-loving. A real free spirit. I loved her more than I had ever loved anyone in my life."

"And then you were hurt more than you'd ever been in your life too," Nina said, her words hushed, as if she was thinking about that fact. "Do you have a picture of her?"

I pulled out my wallet and took out the only thing I had left to remember Natalia by. "This was taken only a few days before the wreck." I pushed it to Nina.

She picked it up and looked at it. "She's beautiful, Ashton. I'm so sorry that it all ended the way it did."

"We were only a few weeks away from the wedding date when it happened." My gut clenched as I recalled it. "It began to rain, and the day had been hot. The police said that the oil had pooled on the pavement and then mixed with the rain, and that's what made me lose control of the car. Everyone said it wasn't my fault, including her family. But I blamed myself. I still do."

"But you shouldn't." She slid the picture back to me. "I'm sure Natalia would hate for you to blame yourself for an accident. She did love you, after all, Ashton."

Looking at Nina, I saw her in a new light. There had always been an attraction between us, but I wasn't ready to go down that road again. Somehow though, the way she was talking to me made me feel closer to her than I had been to anyone since Natalia.

Tapping the top of my desk, Nina got up. "Well, we've got work to get to. Did you really enjoy the coffee?"

"I really did. And the conversation, Nina. I haven't talked about her with anyone in such a long time," I found myself admitting to her. "I feel a little freer, having spoken to you."

"Good. Feel free to talk to me about her—or anything else— anytime you want to. I think I'll be stopping by with some fresh coffee for you from now on." She waved as she opened the door to leave. "Bye. Will I see you at lunch?"

"You will. I'm thinking cheesesteaks." I put Natalia's picture back in my wallet.

"Yum. Sounds good." She left my office, and I was left staring after her.

What just happened here?

CHAPTER THREE

Nina

A week of stopping by Ashton's office with a cup of my magical coffee and I thought things were going well. We didn't have any more talks about the fiancée he'd lost, but we did have small little chats about subjects we'd never discussed before.

Things like which season of the year we each liked the best. It turned out that we were both lovers of the fall. I liked the cool weather, finding it a relief from the heat of summer. Ashton liked it better because of all of the colors of leaves.

It was spring then, nowhere near the fall, but I found myself suggesting that he take a driving trip once the colors began to change. He only shook his head, then let me know that he didn't like to take scenic drives anymore. I left it at that.

He had told me that the weather was hot the day of his accident. I knew it wasn't in the fall, so that did give me hope that one day he and I might be able to take a drive some fall afternoon in the future. I could always be the driver if he wasn't up to it.

Ashton needed to get back to living a full life. It was becoming more and more apparent that it only looked like he was living a normal life from the outside. He seemed fun and social at work, but having these more in-depth talks made me realize that wasn't the full picture. It was when he wasn't at work that worried me.

What does he do when he leaves the station?

That was on my mind a lot. I pictured him smiling as he did most nights as we all left to head home after a long day at work. We all went our separate ways, catching cabs, or walking to the subway station, or getting on buses. We all had places to go, and most of us had other people there when we got home. Ashton didn't, and that made my heart hurt for the man.

I had talked to my roommate Kyle about why a man would want to live alone. Kyle was about Ashton's age, around thirty. He'd been married and had a son that he got every other weekend, so I knew he would empathize with what Ashton was going through.

I was only 23 and had never lost anyone I had loved, not that I had ever really been in love. Tommy Smith in high school couldn't be called real love. That was teenage lust, at best. And I'd never gone out with any guy in college more than a time or two. What Ashton was going through was completely foreign to me.

Kyle had told me that Ashton probably just didn't like to be around people very much and that he liked the break from everyone when he went home. He said quite a few people who were outgoing, fun-loving, and really social could also be introverts, needing downtime to replenish themselves.

I didn't think Ashton needed downtime, though. I thought there had to be something else. But I couldn't put my finger on it, other than that he really didn't want to be hurt by losing another person he loved.

But I had hope that little by little, I was beginning to get under his skin, bringing me a little closer to his heart. That's the place I wanted to get into. I wanted to set up camp and live there with the man who took up space in my thoughts more often than not.

As bad as I wanted things to progress between us, I played my hand nice and slow. Something told me that Ashton Lange could not be rushed into anything. He was very nice on the outside, but I had a feeling that if you tried to dig too deeply that he could turn into a fierce animal, protecting his vulnerable underbelly. The thought made me sad at times.

One would never suspect the strong, virile man of housing such sadness, guilt, and pain. Not that he ever really showed me that side of him, either. No matter how he tried to hide it, I could see it at times. Now that we were talking more about things that were more personal than what we wanted to eat or what was going on at work, I could see things in his eyes.

Those gorgeous cerulean eyes of his could hold joy and laughter in them, and most would only see that. I was getting to where I could see behind that now. And what I saw frightened me. I saw sheer will and determination to keep everyone at arm's length. As if he thought that if he trusted someone enough to get close, then something terrible might happen.

Again.

It would take a lot of time for me to get where I wanted to be with the man. But I was willing to put it in. There was so much about Ashton that was good and right that it would be well worth my time to get him to see that love wasn't something to be afraid of.

I sat at my desk on a Friday afternoon, looking out the little window in my small office. I had a desk, a laptop computer, and a chair to sit in. No other furniture was necessary for me to do my job.

Not one to have too many things around to clutter up my space, I liked the clean look of my office. The cleaning staff would be in later to dust and vacuum, so I closed my computer and put it in the top drawer of my desk before locking it up. Done with the social media part of my job, I didn't need the computer again until Monday morning.

I had no plans for the weekend—nothing unusual there. My other roommate, Sandy, was a party animal who was always inviting me out. I'd go with her every now and then, but usually ended up regretting it. She called me a stick in the mud on all those occasions. Not that I cared.

Sandy didn't believe in making commitments. That meant she

had no problem seeing whomever she wanted, whenever she wanted. I didn't judge her for her choices, but that life wasn't for me.

Turning around in my chair, I found Julia leaning on my door-frame. "What's up?"

She looked me up and down. "You look bored, Nina."

"I'm fine." I didn't like anyone feeling sorry for me. If I told Julia that I was thinking about the lame weekend I had before me, then she would make it her mission to find something for me to do.

"Oh, really?" She rolled her eyes. "Well, I've got a question to ask you. Do you have time in your busy schedule to answer it for me?"

With a laugh, I answered, "Sure, I can make time for your question. Shoot."

"What are your plans for this weekend?" She looked at her nails, then polished them on her shirt.

I thought that was an odd question coming from her. She and Artimus always made plans for their weekends. So why would she be asking me about mine? "Not much. Why?"

Her dark brown eyes lit up. "Good. So, you're free?"

"Maybe." I wasn't about to let her think I would do anything she wanted. Mostly because I had no idea if I would like it or not. "What do you have going on?"

"A little fun for my friends and me." She winked at me. "How about you come out to our home in the Hamptons for the weekend? We can get the limo to drive us there and it'll be so much fun. Please say yes, Nina."

I wasn't about to commit just yet. "Who is *we*?" I arched one brow as I saw her smile get even bigger.

"We, us, the normal group we hang in. Artimus, of course. Duke and Lila too. You know, our little pack." She put her hand on her hip. "So, are you in? We're leaving work early, and I've already got you covered."

"You do?" I was astonished that she would do something like that without consulting me first. "While I'm glad to have the night off as well as the weekend, I'm going to have to say no. I don't want to be the fifth wheel in your double date."

Her dark eyebrows wiggled as she smiled at me with a grin I'd never seen on her before. "Oh, we're not a foursome. You won't be the fifth wheel."

I looked at her with even more suspicion. "I don't get it."

"I can see that." She giggled and clapped. "This is so much fun. I had no idea how fun it would be."

"Julia!" I got out of my chair to walk over to her. "You're not making any sense. Can you get to the point already?"

"Ashton is coming too." She threw her hands up in the air as if she'd done a magic trick. "There it is, Nina. Ashton is coming with us."

"Why?" I asked her, and then added as a thought came to me, "Does he know you invited me too?"

She nodded. "Yes, he does. You see, Artimus invited him without telling me anything about it. I had no idea he even wanted to have people over this weekend. He sprang this on me just a little while ago."

I had this terrible idea that she was trying to play matchmaker and that Ashton had no idea what she was up to. "No way, Julia. I will not put myself in that kind of a position. How embarrassing would it be if Ashton didn't know I was coming and didn't even want me there?"

"Pretty damn embarrassing, I bet," Julia nodded in agreement. "Thank goodness you don't have to worry about that."

"And why wouldn't I need to worry about that?" I looked at her hand as she rested it on my shoulder and then used her other hand to pull my face so that I was looking her right in the eyes. "Ashton told Artimus that he would only go if I invited you too."

It took a few seconds for that to register in my brain.

"Huh?" came my dumb reply.

"He wants you there, Nina." Julia gave my shoulder a squeeze. "If you don't go, he won't go. Those were his exact words to my husband. So, are you in or are you out? I need to let Artimus know what to tell his friend."

Ashton wants me to spend the weekend with him?

"Why didn't he ask me this himself?" I asked her.

She rolled her eyes. "Duh. Because he's Ashton Lange. A man who doesn't date. Or hasn't dated for a long time, anyway. If he had platonic intentions, he probably would've talked to you himself, don't you think?" She lifted her eyebrow at me, as if in challenge, before continuing on in a rush, "Don't answer that though. Don't overthink things—and don't ask so many questions. Just give me the answer I know you want to give me. Say yes so we can get this party going."

"So we'd all head out to your home in a limo together?" I asked.

She nodded. "And on Sunday evening it will bring you guys back home. Friday and Saturday night you'll stay with us, doing all kinds of fun things. It'll be a blast." She ran her arm around my shoulders, pulling me close. "And you and Ashton will finally get a chance to see where things can go."

"He really said he wouldn't go unless I went?" I had to ask, just to be sure.

"He did." She ran her finger over my shoulder as she pulled her hand away from me. "So, what do I tell Artimus, Nina?"

"Tell him that I would love to join you guys for the weekend and I appreciate the invitation."

She furrowed her brow. "Is there a 'but' coming?"

Shaking my head, I laughed. "No. There's not a but coming. I would love to come and appreciate the invitation, silly. Now tell me what kind of clothes I should bring. I want to look my best all weekend long if Ashton is going to be there."

My chance had come, and I wasn't going to let it go to waste.

CHAPTER FOUR

Ashton

With my bags packed and ready to go, all I had to do was sit and wait for Artimus and the others to arrive in the limousine. I sipped on a rum and Coke to help dull the nervous edge I couldn't shake.

I really had no idea where the words had come from when Artimus had asked me if I wanted to spend the weekend with him and his wife as well as Duke and Lila. I'd said I would, but only if Nina came along too.

He'd agreed immediately, a wide smile on his face as he'd punched me in the arm, calling me an old dog for some reason.

I believed the fact that Nina and I had been friends for so long was the reason I had so many reservations about what I'd gotten myself into. I didn't want to lose her as a friend if I couldn't do the romantic relationship thing with her. I didn't think I could do it with anyone, and I didn't want her to think it wasn't anything against her.

If I could figure it out again, Nina would most definitely be the woman I'd choose to dive into those dark and treacherous waters with. Waters I knew I wasn't ready to jump into.

So that's why I kept mulling over why I'd given Artimus that ultimatum in the first place. If I couldn't get into anything romantic with Nina, then what the hell was I doing making sure she was going to be with me all weekend?

Nothing I did was making much sense to me. And it had all started with Nina bringing me that first cup of coffee. Somehow that first conversation had opened a gate that had been closed for many years, locked up tight, never to be re-opened. But she'd managed to open it without me even realizing what she was doing. I doubted she even realized the effect she'd had on me these last couple weeks.

When my cell buzzed with a text from Artimus telling me they were pulling up to my building, I picked up my suitcase and headed out the door. My heart was racing because I knew I was about to embark on a journey I wasn't ready for in the least.

When I got to the car, the driver opened the door, and I saw everyone inside except for Nina. "She changed her mind?"

Julia and Lila laughed while Duke and Artimus grinned at me. "We're picking her up last, lover-boy. No need to worry," Artimus teased.

The driver put my bag in the trunk as I slipped into the large car, scowling at my so-called friends. "I would rather you not call me that, Artimus."

I felt like a kid in junior high whose friends were setting him up or something. Only I was the one who'd asked for Nina to be invited —they hadn't had anything to do with it. My head was all over the place, and apparently, it showed.

Julia opened the fridge of the minibar and tossed me a cold beer. "Here, have one of these, Ashton. It'll help calm those nerves."

I opened the bottle as I asked, "Does it really show that much?"

Lila nodded. "Yep. You shouldn't be nervous. Nina really likes you."

I knew she did. I wasn't nervous about that. I was just nervous about everything else.

The beer helped a bit, and when we stopped at Nina's apartment building, I was feeling a little more confident. Julia pulled out her phone. "I'll just text her real quick."

"No, let me go get her." I pushed the door open. "Um, does anyone know what the apartment number is?"

"Six seventy-five," Lila told me.

I headed out of the car and went up to the sixth floor. My palms were sweaty, my stomach tight, my head felt like there was a balloon in there instead of a brain, but I was doing it.

I got to the door and rang the bell then wiped my hands on my jeans and shook my head to clear it. When a man about my age opened the door, I just about freaked out. "Hey!"

He stood tall, looking me up and down. "And you are?"

I stuck my hand out. "Ashton Lange. And you are?"

"Kyle." He shook my hand. "What can I do for you?"

"I'm here for Nina." I gulped as he let my hand go. His dark eyes pierced me as he eyed me. She had never said a word about any man who might be staying with her. "Do you live here?"

"Yep," came his response.

"With Nina?" I asked.

"Yep." He stepped back. "She's in the bathroom. You can wait here if you want to." He walked away, shouting, "Nina, someone's here for you."

The man was big and bulky. His dark hair was cut short. I didn't really see him as Nina's type. But I guessed he had to be if they were living together.

All of my newfound confidence and determination about trying to take things further with Nina crashed into the pit of my stomach. I'd thought we'd be on the same page about this little weekend getaway, but obviously we weren't if she was with someone else.

Maybe they had an open relationship. Or maybe she just wanted to stay friends. Whatever it was, I was feeling mighty jealous.

A door opened, and Nina came out of the bathroom, running her hands over her dress. Lilac lace covered a purple silk short sundress, and she had no shoes on. "Ashton, you didn't have to come up to get me."

"I didn't mind doing it." I jerked my head toward the man who stood in the kitchen, looking inside the fridge. "And who's he?"

"Kyle?" she asked.

I nodded. "And what's he to you?" It came out sounding much gruffer than I'd have liked, but I couldn't stop myself.

"My roommate," she said, looking at me like I had mush for brains—and I couldn't blame her in that moment—before walking to her bedroom. "Let me grab my bag."

I looked at Kyle, and he grinned at me as he raised his dark brows. "I had to give you the business, dude."

With a shrug, I said, "Did you?"

Nina came out with her bag in hand and I immediately took it from her. "You don't have to ..."

"I want to," I told her as we headed to the door.

The elevator wasn't far from her door, and it was nearly full of people when the doors opened for us. She and I didn't say so much as one word all the way down. Then we walked out of the building, still not saying a thing.

Was this how the weekend would be, the two of us together in awkward silence?

The driver put her bag in the back and we got into the car. There were three bench-type seats, one along the back, and the other two on each side. Duke and Lila sat on one side, Julia and Artimus sat on the back seat. That left the other seat free, and Nina and I took it.

Lila leaned forward, two beers in her hands. "Here ya go."

We both took the drinks she offered, and I couldn't help but notice how we were both quick to take sips. It seemed she was as nervous as I was. And I didn't like that.

I always tried to make everyone around me feel comfortable. So, my nerves took a backseat as I focused on making Nina feel relaxed. Sitting back, I laid my arm on the back of the seat behind her. "So, besides that guy, who else lives in that apartment with you?"

"Sandy. It's just us three—Kyle, Sandy, and me." She took another drink as she sat back and got comfortable, which was a relief to see. "We like having Kyle living there. He's like our guard dog."

"I didn't know you had a male roomie, Nina," Lila said, looking a little confused. "What else have you been keeping a secret from us, your best friends?"

Nina laughed, the sound tickling my ears and making me smile. "I didn't think it was a secret. I don't recall anyone ever asking me about my roommates, so the particulars on that subject never came up."

I took the opportunity to learn more about her life. "So, tell us about the people you live with."

She turned her head to look at me. "Really? That's kind of boring."

"Not to me, it's not." I moved my hand to rest on her shoulder. "I want to know about your life outside of work."

With a shrug, she went on, "Sandy is a couple of years older than I am. I hope I'm a bit more settled down at 25 than she is. She's quite the party animal. Kyle is a thirty-something divorcee with a young son he gets every other weekend. Kyle doesn't go out much; he's kind of reclusive since the divorce. He caught his wife cheating and doesn't trust himself to pick the right kind of woman."

"He's got a kid, huh?" I felt kind of bad for the guy then. And I found myself wondering what would have happened to me if Natalia and I had already had a child when she died. Would things have been different with me? Would I have dealt with things differently if I had a child to care for?

Nina's hand on my leg stole my thoughts, and I looked down at it as it rested on my thigh. "His situation is different than yours, Ashton. Don't try to compare them."

How did she know what I was thinking?

I shook my head as I looked at her. "Can you read my mind or something?"

Lila laughed. "Your face told all of us what you were thinking. You're kind of an open book—when you don't realize that anyone is looking at you, that is."

Everyone in that car had only known each other for two years, and yet we all knew each other very well. It was almost as if we'd been friends forever.

Nina moved her hand and took another drink of the beer before saying, "So, what are we going to do tonight in the Hamptons, Julia?"

She jerked a thumb toward Artimus. "Ask the master of ceremonies here. I don't have a clue."

Artimus was quick to respond. "Tonight we're having a game night. Charades, Pictionary, then strip poker."

Nina nearly choked on her sip of beer. "I'm out of that last one!"

Artimus had a good laugh. "No, everyone is in. We'll make it interesting by bulking everyone up in lots of clothing. The first one down to their original clothes loses the game. And you girls get to learn how to play poker, so you can start joining us for our weekly poker nights. Us guys miss you girls on those nights. It'll be a fun activity we can all do together."

Julia smiled at her husband. "You miss me when you play poker, babe?"

He kissed the tip of her nose. "I do."

Watching them, I got a funny feeling deep in my heart. That feeling felt a little too much like loneliness—like I was missing out on something that I'd stubbornly refused to dwell on.

It sounded to me like Artimus had a bonding weekend planned, and that meant Nina and I would be subjected to activities that would bring us even closer than we already were.

And as great as that sounded, it also sounded kind of horrifying to me.

5

CHAPTER FIVE

Nina

Artimus' game night proved to be fun for all. I wasn't any good at playing poker, so I was the one who lost that game. I was thankful for the many layers of clothing Artimus provided for us, or I would've been bare-assed right in front of all of them.

Saturday morning had me waking up in the bedroom next to Ashton's. It was a little awkward when the other couples headed off to bed and he and I walked down the long hallway to our separate bedrooms.

I thought he was about to kiss me the night before, but in the end, he merely pulled my hand to his lips and kissed the top of it before telling me he had a great time and wishing me a good night.

My sleep was pretty good. I dreamt about him, and that was almost as good as getting to be with the real man. After a couple of years of dreams and fantasies about Ashton, I'd resigned myself to the fact that that was likely as much as I'd ever have.

But now I had a perfect opportunity right in front of me, and I was going to make something happen. I wanted a real kiss from him.

And I was going to do my best to entice him into giving me that kiss in any way I could.

We passed a pleasant morning together, taking a leisurely breakfast and lingering over our coffees before parting ways and then reconvening for lunch. I'd headed up to my bedroom to freshen up after lunch when I heard a knock at my door. Ashton called out through the closed door, "Hey, we're all going down to the pool. Put on your bathing suit and meet us down there, Nina."

"Okay. Give me a minute." I went to get my suit out of my suitcase.

"Sure thing. I'll see you down there." He left my door, and I looked at the two piece I'd pulled out.

It wasn't daring or especially sexy. Just a regular royal blue bikini, but it was all I had. "Why haven't I ever invested in a sexy swimsuit?" I muttered to myself with regret.

Here it was—my time to shine and show off my body for Ashton, and all I had was a humdrum bathing suit. I knew Lila and Julia would both be wearing something hot and sexy.

With no other choice, I put the thing on and wrapped myself in a white towel before heading downstairs to the indoor pool room. I heard splashing and laughing as I got closer.

When I stepped inside, I saw there was a volleyball net strung up, separating the two halves of the pool. They were playing girls against boys.

Ashton was sitting on the edge, waiting for me to arrive so we could join them together. "Great, you're here, Nina. Come on." He jumped into the pool, and I walked gracefully down the steps and into the water.

Julia and Lila had chosen the shallower water near the steps, which I was glad for. "Okay, so what's the score so far?" I asked them.

"Boys three, girls one," Lila said. "I hope you can bring some heat, Nina."

Cracking my knuckles, I informed them, "I was on the high school volleyball team. I was dubbed the spike queen." I looked at the three men on the other side of the net. "I hope you guys are ready to get your butts kicked."

They laughed as we all got into position, then Ashton served the ball over to us. Lila made a successful volley back to them, and Artimus sent it back our way. Julia managed to hit it back over, then Ashton came splashing forward, hitting it back, making it just over the net.

I saw my shot. "Lila, set."

She hit the ball up high into the air, and I jumped up, spiking it over the net with my fist.

SMACK!

"Shit!" Ashton shouted. "Ow!"

"Nina?" Artimus yelled.

The glory was all gone as I saw blood in the water. The ball had hit Ashton right in the nose. "God! Ashton, I'm so sorry!" I swam under the net to get to him. Blood was running in rivers out from under his hand, which was covering his nose.

"It's okay," he said with a high, nasally tone to his normally deep voice.

"No, it's not." I felt terrible. No, worse than terrible. I felt sick that I had done that to him. "Come on. This is my fault; I'll take care of you."

Julia handed me a dark red towel as we all got out of the pool. "Here, use this to put pressure on his nose. That should stop the bleeding."

The guys helped Ashton to a lounge chair and laid him back, and I took a seat next to him. "Move your hands and I'll use this towel to stop the bleeding."

When he pulled his hands away, I gasped.

"Shit! Is it that bad?" he asked.

It was awful. "No. No," I lied as I put the towel on his nose very gently." I looked at Julia. "Do you think you can get me a little baggie of ice?"

She nodded. "Damn, that's going to leave a mark."

Ashton's eyes were bloodshot as he looked at me and asked, "It is?"

I tried to downplay it. "It's going to be all right. No reason to worry."

After Julia came back with the ice, the others headed inside to change. Pool-time fun was over, and it was all my fault. My eyes must've conveyed how guilty I felt because Ashton took me by the wrist. "It was an accident, Nina. Don't look so guilt-stricken. I'll be okay. Sure, a little bruised and battered, but I'll get over that."

Biting my lip as I pulled the towel back to see if the bleeding had stopped, I found I had hit him high up on the bridge of his nose. Both eyes would surely turn black, but it didn't seem to be broken. "At least there's no bone jutting out. That's a good sign."

"I would say so." He laughed then stopped abruptly. "Ouch. Don't make me laugh. It hurts."

"Noted. No funny stuff with you for the rest of the day." Covering the plastic bag of ice with a hand towel Julia had brought with it, I placed it on the bridge of his nose. "If you keep this on for a while, I think it will lessen the swelling."

"It's so cold," he whimpered.

Leaning over him, I kissed his cheek. "I really am sorry, Ashton."

Even bloodshot, his cerulean eyes were still gorgeous as he looked into mine. "Don't be. It got you this close to me. That can't be a bad thing. Not in my book."

There were so many things I wanted to ask him, to tell him. But I knew that now wasn't the time to do it. I just had to let the moment be for now.

"I think we can move you, now that the bleeding has stopped. You're going to want a shower. I'll help you get to your room." I got up and took his hand, helping him up too.

He wrapped his arm around my shoulders, and I wrapped mine around his waist to make sure he was steady. "Thanks, Nina. I am a little woozy."

We headed inside and then up the stairs. He stumbled a little, and I felt his arm go tighter around me. "You okay, Ashton?"

We stopped for a moment. "Yeah, I'm okay now. My head just got really light right there." He looked at me, then smiled as he held the ice on his nose. "I'm not entirely sure if it was from the injury or this." His arm tightened around me even more. "I kind of like this."

"The pain?" I asked, thinking he was crazy. I had heard about people liking the euphoria that happened after an injury as the adrenaline rushed to the brain.

"No, silly girl." He took another step up. "Holding you. You, holding me."

My face heated as I blushed. Ashton had never talked to me that way before. It was so odd, even though I had wanted him to see me as more than just a friend for a long time. It was just a little weird.

And when I didn't say anything back as we kept walking, I felt his hold on me loosen. When we got to his bedroom door, he moved his arm off my shoulders.

"I'm going to shower and change. If you need me to help you back down ..."

"That's okay, Nina. I think I can handle it from here." He went into his room without looking at me at all.

My silence had been a stupid move on my part. I stood there, looking at his closed door and wondering if I should just go inside and tell him that I was happy holding him too.

But I didn't do that. I just stood there for a solid five minutes before turning and going to my bedroom. Stripping the bathing suit away from my body as I walked toward the attached bathroom, I wondered why I had reacted like that.

It was proving harder for me than I'd thought to go from friends to more than friends after all this time. I had watched what I said to Ashton for so long, keeping my feelings from him was like second nature to me.

All kinds of silent words of affection had gone through my mind over the years as the two of us had talked. I had kept those words to myself, and it seemed that was a habit I was going to have trouble breaking.

But I knew I had to, if I ever wanted to hear Ashton say something like that again.

Turning on the shower, I cranked it so it was steaming hot, then got in and let the water run over me. Moving my hands all over my body, I recalled just how often I had done that and imagined them to be Ashton's hands instead of my own.

I couldn't count all the times I'd pushed my fingers deep into my cunt, fantasizing that they were Ashton's thick fingers inside of me. I could touch myself, pretending it was him, but I couldn't find words to say when he told me he liked how it felt for us to hold each other.

The water pressure eased up for a moment, and I realized that Ashton was naked right on the other side of that wall. He was in the shower in his room, lathering his muscular body with soap and probably internally berating himself for saying anything to me about how he felt.

I was filled with even more guilt at that thought. Not only had I messed up his gorgeous face, but I had also hurt his pride. I had made him feel like a fool by not saying a word back to him.

It had felt good to me too, to have his arm around me and mine around him. Sparks had been flying through me with us being that close. My body had heated up, and my mind had already been moving ahead to other things.

Perhaps that's why I couldn't think of anything to say after he'd told me that. Or maybe I was just one dumb chick who didn't know how to act when someone said something so sweet to them.

Whatever it was, I was going to fix it. I was going to get dressed, then go find him and tell him that I liked how it felt too and I was just too stupid to know how to put it.

I leaned my back against the tiled wall, knowing he was right behind me on the other side. "Ashton, I'm sorry I'm such an idiot where you're concerned. I hope you can understand. I hope what I did didn't ruin whatever it is that you had planned when you thought about us being here this weekend."

Shutting off the water, I got out of the shower and began to dry off. I could hear the water in the next room go off too. And then I heard a weird yelp. "Fuck me!" Ashton's voice came through the wall. "I look like I've been hit with a baseball bat!"

I wouldn't say he looked that bad.

CHAPTER SIX

Ashton

I couldn't stop staring at my face in the mirror. Even with my reflection fogged up from the hot shower I'd just taken, I could see I didn't look quite as good as I had before.

Not at all what I wanted for this weekend.

I wondered if Artimus would see fit to have a masquerade party instead of whatever he had planned. At least then I could hide my face behind a mask.

The thought that I'd come on to Nina while in this state had me feeling more embarrassed than I had ever been.

No wonder she had nothing to say back to me when I told her I liked holding her. I look like a beast!

How could I face her now? How could I fix this whole situation?

On top of looking like I'd been in a fight with Mike Tyson, I had a raging headache too. When I looked through the drawers of the vanity I found all kinds of things, but no pain reliever of any kind.

Going back out to the bedroom, I spied something on the floor by the door. When I walked over, I saw that it was a little note and a sleeve of some pills. Nina had slid them to me. The note said to take two and come down to the patio out back, as Artimus was barbecuing.

Wasting no time, I punched two of the little blue pills out of their aluminum pouches before going to the mini fridge to grab a bottle of water to wash them down with. I decided that lying down on the bed for a little while might help. It would definitely give the pills some time to kick in. And with the bag of ice placed back on my face, I would hopefully get back to feeling and looking kind of human soon.

I hoped.

I must've dozed off because the sound of knocking woke me up. "Ashton, are you okay in there?" came Nina's voice.

Blinking a few times, I finally woke completely up. "Yeah. I'll be down soon."

"Okay," she said. "Just checking on you. It's been over an hour."

I had no idea it had been so long. "I fell asleep. I'll get ready and be right down."

"Did you get the pills I put under the door?" she asked. "They should help with the pain."

"I got them and took them, thanks." I had laid down without a stitch of clothing on and sat up a bit too fast in my effort to put something on and join them. "Whoa!"

"Whoa, what, Ashton?" She tapped the door once more. "Do you need my help?"

In more ways than you know.

"I'll be okay. I just moved too fast is all. I'll be right down, Nina."

"Okay, then." I heard her leaving and finally got out of bed.

When I looked in the mirror, I was still unhappy with my appearance. A bruise had begun to form underneath my right eye, which seemed to have gotten the brunt of the ball.

"So, stay on her right. Then all she'll see is your left side." I turned to see how that would look in the mirror and thought it wasn't the worst idea I'd ever had.

With a plan in mind, I put on some shorts and a T-shirt, then padded out of the room in my bare feet. Shoving my hands through my hair, I felt like I was as presentable as I could manage to get myself, given the circumstances.

The sound of laughter and clinking glasses easily led me to my friends on the back patio. The smell of the pit helped me find my way too. "There he is," Duke said as he came to me. He stopped to grab a beer out of the cooler and brought it to me. "Here ya go. I bet you could use a nice cold one, Ashton."

"I could." I opened it and took a long drink as I scanned the area for Nina. But she wasn't there. "Do you happen to know where Nina is?"

He jerked his head toward the right. "She went to check out the flower garden. It's that way."

So that's the way I went. "I'll be back."

Duke called out after me, "No need to rush back. The food won't be ready for quite a while."

Rounding the corner, I caught Nina running her hand over the petals of a white rose. I stood there for a moment, just looking at her. She'd put on a white sundress, her hair pulled back into a high ponytail, and she didn't have any makeup on at all.

And she'd never looked more beautiful to me.

When her eyes left the rose, they moved to me. "I see you've decided to join us." She came straight to me, her hand gently running over my cheek.

"I know, it's horrible." I shoved one hand into my pocket as I looked away. "I'm a wreck."

"I wasn't going to say that at all." She ran her hand down my arm, leaving a trail of tingles in her wake. "I was going to say that you're already looking much better."

"Ah, so you've decided to lie to me about it, then. I see the route you're taking. Classy, Nina. Very classy." I took a drink of the beer as I eyed her.

"I wouldn't call it lying, Ashton." She blinked her long, thick lashes at me.

"Being polite is probably what you would call it." I recalled what I had said to her and thought it might be the right time to bring that up. "I'm sorry I said that to you when we were heading up the stairs. I put you on the spot, and I wanted you to know that I didn't mean to make you feel uncomfortable or anything."

Her expression turned awkward. "Oh, that. No problem. I mean, I should apologize for my lack of words. I just didn't know what to say."

I chuckled. "I bet you wanted to say that I was a hideous beast at that moment and it wasn't the right time to be making any moves on anyone. I don't want you to worry. I've put myself in check, now that I'm disfigured."

She laced her arm through mine and began to walk through the garden. "You're much more than just a pretty face, Ashton. You've got a sparkling personality too, you know."

"Sparkling?" I laughed. "I had no idea." I was thankful she'd moved to my left side.

She took a deep sniff of a yellow flower. "Oh, that one smells nice." Then she looked up at me with her cheeks going red. "God, I'm sorry, Ashton."

"Why?" I had to ask her, as I had no idea why she would be sorry.

"Because you probably can't smell anything since I smashed you in the nose with that ball and here I am talking about how things smell. It's rude of me." She looked around at all the flowers as I laughed at her. "Come on, let's go see what's going on with everyone else."

But I didn't want to go be around everyone else. I liked being with her and just her. So I found something else we could do alone. Pointing to the path I saw leading into the woods, I asked, "Want to see where that trail leads?"

Her narrow shoulders moved with a shrug. "Why not?"

We headed in that direction, and I was happy to have her to myself for a little while longer.

Nina and I went to lunch together a lot, but there were usually other people with us. As much time as we'd spent together in the past couple years, we hadn't spent much of it alone. And suddenly, all I wanted was for us to be alone.

I pulled a tree branch back at the beginning of the trail and let her go in front of me. "Ladies first."

She stepped ahead. "Good. I've always heard that if there's a snake on a trail, it'll bite the second person, not the first." She looked back at me with a grin. "So, watch out." When she turned back around, I noticed that she shivered. "It's dark in here."

"It is." I looked around at the thick foliage surrounding us. "Do you think there're bats in here?"

She stopped and turned to look at me. "Are you kidding? Do they even have bats in the Hamptons, Ashton?"

"I was kidding, Nina." I was just trying to scare her, but I didn't think that would really do the trick. "Are you a big chicken?"

"No," came her quick reply. "Just cautious is all." She stopped abruptly and pointed at a black stick on the ground ahead of us. "Is that a snake?" She moved back until her back hit my front—and my front was suddenly very happy about her skittishness.

I put my arms around her, holding her. "I'm not sure." The smell of her hair was intoxicating—honey and lemons would forever be etched into my brain with her image. "Should I take the lead?"

She scrambled around behind me, then pushed at my lower back. "Yes. Please do."

I loved the way she held onto my waist, peeking around me. "I'm pretty sure it's just a stick, Nina. Nothing to be afraid of."

"It looked like it moved to me." Her hands clamped my sides harder. "Just be careful, okay?"

When we got to the stick, I stopped, leaned over to pick it up, and showed it to her. "See, just a stick."

For some reason, she still looked concerned about it. "Yeah, that's a stick, but look what's on it, Ashton. Drop it!" She backed away from me as she stared at it.

"For Pete's sake, Nina." I turned the stick around and found a spider was crawling up it, making its way to my fingers. "Shit!" I chucked the thing—spider and all—as far away from us as my arm could manage.

Nina laughed as she came back to me. "See, I told you that stick was something to be concerned about. That spider almost bit you. Adding a spider bite to your other injuries wouldn't be a good idea."

"Maybe this hike through the jungle isn't a good idea either." I looked ahead at the path as she moved past me to forge ahead.

"Come on. I want to see where we end up." Taking the lead once more, Nina was set on seeing this through.

Following her, I liked the view as her plump ass moved beneath the soft fabric of her dress. Neither of us was wearing shoes, and the cool grass felt like heaven on my bare feet. "This is nice, being out here, communing with nature."

She turned to look at me as she walked backward. "It does feel nice out here. I haven't done anything like this in forever. It feels freeing, in a way."

And just like that, she tripped on something and fell flat on her ass. "Nina!" I rushed to help her up as she sat there, looking stunned. "Are you okay?"

I pulled her up and dusted her off, my hand moving back and forth over her butt. Then I saw her cheeks turning red, and she moved back a few steps. "I'm fine. It just startled me, is all."

"Your white dress has green grass stains across the back of it now. I guess we should head back so you can change and get that thing soaking before the stain sets in. Grass stains are one of the hardest ones to get out." I took her hand, leading her back in the direction of the house.

I caught her smiling. "You do your own laundry?"

"I do." I smiled right back at her. "And if you give me that dress after you take it off, then I can make sure to get that stain out, so it doesn't get ruined."

After all these years, I was finally getting Nina out her dress— albeit for a much less satisfying reason than I'd been dreaming about.

CHAPTER SEVEN

Nina

The sound of a grandfather clock chiming the hour later that night had the girls and me settling into a game of Scrabble as the guys played their beloved poker. They'd taught us how to play the night before, but it was apparent our constant questions were getting in the way of their fun. We thought we'd give them some free time and entertain ourselves for a while.

Lila laid down the word 'zebra.' "And that gives me 16 points," she said.

I laughed as I used her 'z' to make a new word, worth even more points. "'Zephyr.' And that's 23 points for me. Ha!"

Julia looked at her tiles, pulling her lips to one side as she tried to beat us. "Okay, let me see here. I'm going to use the 'y' in zephyr to make the word 'why.' And that will give me twelve points."

I had to give her kudos. "Not bad for only using three letters, Julia."

"I thought so too." She patted herself on the back. "So, how're things progressing between you and Ashton?"

With a sigh, I wondered the same thing myself. "I don't know. He did say something that led me to believe that he would like things to go in a more romantic direction. But then I just went completely blank on him."

Lila plopped down some tiles under the 'p' in zephyr. "'Phrase.' And that'll give me 11 points." Her eyes turned to mine. "You went blank on him? What does that mean?"

"It means that he told me he liked the way it felt, us holding each other." I decided I needed to clarify that. "I was helping him up the stairs. He had his arm around my shoulders, and I had mine around his waist, to support him."

Julia frowned at me. "And you went blank on him?"

"Yeah." I shook my head as I looked at the floor. "I just didn't know what to say."

Lila laughed. "That's easy, Nina. You say, 'I like this too.' And then you guys kiss, and it's all smooth sailing from there." She threw her arms up in the air. "Why do you two make this so hard? It's as easy as pie, really."

"That's where you're wrong," I told her. "It's not easy. You see, he told me about his fiancée. He told me how she'd been the only woman he'd ever loved. And I think he still loves her."

Julia, who was always much more spiritual than either of us, chimed in, "I'm sure he does still love her. But she's incapable of being there for him now. You are very capable, and you need to show him that."

I put two tiles down, using the existing 'w' to make the word, 'wow.' "Nine points for 'wow.'" Then I looked at Julia with a stoic expression. "Julia, what if I told you that I don't like competing for a man?"

Nodding, she said, "I would say that's fine. But who is it that you think you're competing with?"

"His dead fiancée, Natalia Reddy."

Julia and Lila both gasped, then Julia asked, "Did he tell you her name?"

"Of course. How else would I know it?" I couldn't understand why they were looking at me with such surprised expressions.

Lila was the first to let me in on things. "Nina, he's never told anyone her name. Not even Duke and Artimus, and they're his best friends."

Julia nodded. "He's trusting you more than he even trusts them. That's huge, Nina."

Considering what they said, I did think it was pretty huge that he would talk to me about the woman he'd loved and lost. "Do you guys think he told me more about her so that I would know just how much he isn't over her yet?"

"What makes you think that he's not over her?" Julia asked.

With a shrug, I said, "I just have this feeling deep inside of me that he's not. And I also think that he's afraid of losing someone like that again. So much so that he would rather be alone than take the risk of getting hurt the way he did."

Lila and Julia exchanged sad looks. Then they both looked at me. Julia was the one to ask, "Are you thinking about giving up on him, Nina?"

Shaking my head, I said, "How could I? Just a few hours ago, he told me he liked the way it felt to hold me. That's progress, people."

They laughed and nodded in agreement. "Progress it is," Lila said.

Julia chimed in, "Especially when you think about how long you guys have known each other."

Lila jabbed me in the ribs with her elbow. "It'll probably take another year before you two actually kiss. But way to hang in there, girl."

It was all fun and games until she said that. Even Julia could see that Lila had gone too far.

My finger began wagging at Lila as if it had a mind of its own. "Now you listen to me, Lila Cofield," I chided. "That man has suffered things that we can't even imagine. And I won't sit idly by and let anyone, not even a very good friend of mine, say anything negative about him."

Lila's blue eyes were as big as saucers as she shook her head. "I didn't mean anything by it. I swear, Nina. I shouldn't have said that. I'm so sorry. You're right. He has lived through a lot. I can't imagine if that had happened to me. If I'd lost Duke before we even really got started, well, that might've just killed me."

"You're damn right, it would've," I let her know. "Okay, apology accepted. Just watch what you say about him from now on."

"I will," she said with her eyes downcast. "I am sorry. You know I would never say anything to hurt him intentionally—he's my friend too."

Julia got up and came to put her hands on my shoulders as she stood behind me. "Seems like you already have Ashton's back, Nina. I think that's a good sign that things will work out for you two."

I patted her hand that rested on my shoulder. "I wish I had the kind of confidence that you do, Julia. You're so sure about things."

Lila smiled at me, then got up. "I think we should go break up the poker game. Then Julia and I will take our men to bed, and you and Ashton can have some time alone. To talk. Or whatever you want to do." With a wink, she headed out.

I got up and followed Julia as we left the room. The men could be heard laughing and teasing each other before we got to the room that Artimus had dubbed the poker room. Artimus called out, "Aces high, boys. Read 'em and weep."

I heard Ashton groan, "Aw, man. You win again."

Duke said with a chuckle, "And the rich only get richer."

Julia led the way, pushing open the door. "Good. Your game is over, I hear."

"Over?" Artimus asked with confusion. "Not hardly."

"I beg to differ," Julia said as she went to her husband. "I need your help, hubby."

Artimus looked at me then Lila. "Can't your friends help you, baby?"

"Not for what I need you for." She ran her hands over his shoulders seductively before leaning in to whisper some choice words for him alone. But from the glow that began to radiate from Artimus' face, we all assumed the words she said were rather dirty.

Duke was quick to get up and grab his wife, gazing deeply into Lila's eyes. "You have anything you need me to do, honey?"

"Now that you mention it, yes," Lila said.

The couples left Ashton and me alone. I smiled as I took a seat. "I can play you. If you want," I told him.

With a deep sexy chuckle, he said, "Only if we use our clothes to bet instead of chips." He must have been recalling the outcome of the strip poker game the night before.

There my finger went again, wagging away at the naughty man. "Ashton, you are one naughty boy, aren't you?"

"Not normally," he said with a sexy grin. "But I'm starting to get there."

There was a twinkle in his eyes that I hadn't seen before. And that twinkle sent sparks shooting all through me. It also sent something else through me—a feeling that I needed to let him know that he could trust me implicitly.

With that in mind, I decided that I wanted to make our relationship a lot deeper with this weekend excursion. And not just sexually, either. I would let that sit in the background for now. What was more important was letting Ashton know that I wanted him for him, and nothing else.

"You know what?" I asked him.

"What?"

Winking at him, I went on, "I'm kind of glad I got to see you with your face messed up."

Even with swollen eyes, his brows rose up high. "What?"

Nodding, I added, "No, really. I'm glad I got to see you this way. It's helped me learn a lot more about how I really feel."

"Feel about what?" he asked, still seeming very confused.

"You." I looked into his eyes, which were a lot smaller than normal due to the swelling. I still saw him in those eyes. I still found him as attractive as I always had. "Even with that one black eye, your swollen, red nose, and that other eye that's puffy, I still think you're the most handsome man I've ever met."

I couldn't believe it when I saw his cheeks flush and his head lower as he grinned like a maniac. "Shut up, Nina. Stop messing with me. I've looked in a mirror—I know I'm hideous."

"No, I mean it, Ashton," I went on. "I suppose it's because you're handsome—or beautiful, really—inside and out. And no matter the damage, the man you truly are shines through."

His eyes came up to meet mine, and he wasn't smiling anymore. "I think you're beautiful inside and out too."

"Glad to see we're on the same page then," I said, to lighten things up. I didn't want things to lead to kissing just yet. I wanted to really lay everything out for him.

I wouldn't have gone this route with anyone I had ever met prior to Ashton Lange. But we needed a firm foundation, or else any relationship we tried for would merely crumble. He needed a little extra time and attention. I could see that.

For a while, he just stared into my eyes before saying, "You're a very good person, Nina. I hope you know that about yourself."

With a shrug, I said, "I'm no better than the next person, Ashton."

He shook his head. "Oh, but you are. I want you to know that. You are much better than most people."

If I didn't know what I did about the man, I would've been jumping up and down. Shouting at him and demanding to know why he hadn't made his move yet, if I was such a great person.

Since I did know about his past and his loss, I wasn't about to do a thing like that. What I was about to do was let him see all of me, and I hoped he would let me in deeper too.

I'd never been one to delve too deeply into a person, but as they say, there's a first time for everything.

8

CHAPTER EIGHT

Artimus

"There's a balcony off my bedroom," Nina said, with a sexy little smile curving her pink lips. "I noticed that your room didn't have one when I walked out on mine earlier today."

I had the idea that she wanted to get me into her bedroom, and that sat pretty well with me. "You noticed that, did ya?"

"I did," she nodded, "and I thought you might like to come up to my bedroom and hang out on it with me. The stars are sure to be shining bright tonight."

Unsure if I was really ready for what was about to happen, I got up and reached out for her hand anyway. "Sure, let's go do a little stargazing, Nina."

"Good." She came along right behind me as I led her up to her room.

I opened her door, finding the room dark. The thought crossed my mind to pull her inside with me, close the door, and pin her against it. Our breaths would mingle in a warm cloud, then our lips would touch, and it would be one of the most magical things I had ever felt.

I knew that without a doubt.

But she foiled my plan when she reached in and pushed the switch to turn on the overhead lights. Silently, I padded toward the balcony doors and thought that I might give the kissing idea a try once we got under the stars.

Pulling the doors open, I felt her hand leave mine. "Go on out there. I've got to use the restroom. I'll be right back."

Foiled again!

Watching her walk away from me, I admired her round backside as I leaned on the doorframe. "Not bad at all," I whispered.

She closed the door behind her, and I turned to check out the balcony. Two chairs were on either side of a small table. Glancing over my shoulder to make sure she wasn't out yet, I hurried to move the chairs away from the table. Placing them side by side, I took a seat and waited for her to join me.

The stars were bright, the night air was cool, and I was up for something different tonight. It was time to make some changes in my life, and this would be the turning point.

Pepping myself up, I told myself that Nina was perfect for me. She had all the qualities I admired in people. She was honest, nice, polite, and it didn't hurt that she was one of the most beautiful young woman I'd ever met.

Knowing that there was no such thing as a perfect person, I tried to think of anything I didn't like about Nina.

Leaning back in my chair, I tapped my chin with my forefinger and thought as hard as I could. "Nope, nothing."

"Who are you talking to, Ashton?" Nina came out and took the seat next to me with a silly grin on her face.

"Um ... Uh ..." I'd been caught. "No one."

With a sweet light laugh that sent me into a daze, she said, "They say only highly intelligent people talk to themselves. Did you know that?"

"I must have. Since I must be highly intelligent." With a chuckle, I put my hands behind my head and leaned back to look up at the night sky. "It's a beautiful night. You were right; sitting out here is a good idea."

Leaning back in her chair, she agreed, "I think so too." She took in a deep breath of the fresh air then turned her head to look at me. "Ashton, what kind of future do you see for yourself?"

So, right to the hard questions, I see.

"Oh, I don't know, Nina." I really didn't. I hadn't thought about my future—well, since the accident. I cut my eyes off to the side as that thought filled my head, the images coming back to the forefront of my mind.

Flames, screams, sirens.

Her hand touched mine, bringing me back to reality. "Ashton. I know you probably haven't let yourself think about the future for a while. Before that terrible thing happened, what kind of future did you see for yourself?"

Looking into her green eyes, I had to ask, "Can you read my mind? I know I've asked you that before, but you're just so spot on, Nina."

"It's in your eyes, Ashton." The pad of her thumb ran back and forth over the top of my hand, making me feel comfortable and relaxed. "And your body language too. So, what were your ideas for the future?"

"A nice home, a wife, and a family." I turned the question back on her. "And what about you, Nina?"

The way she smiled at me made my heart speed up. It was so open and honest. "I've always wanted kids. And who doesn't want a nice home? To be honest, though, I have never given much thought to having a husband."

"I know this isn't a question you're supposed to ask a woman," I was treading into deep water with her, "but how many boyfriends are in your past?"

"You want to know how many men I've had sex with? That's what you're really asking me, right?" She laughed a little awkwardly before continuing. "And that's okay. Understandable, even." She held up one hand. "Less than the fingers on this one hand, if you must know."

Relief filled me with her answer, no matter how illogical I knew that to be. I wasn't a prude, but I couldn't help feeling jealous at the thought of Nina with many other men. "That's not bad at all."

Her brows raised. "And now it's your turn, Ashton."

Oh, no!

Explaining my past hadn't been easy when I'd had to tell Natalia about it. And it wasn't any easier now to tell Nina. "Okay, first of all, you need to know that I am not the same man I was when I was in high school and college. That's the first thing you have to keep in mind when I tell you my answer."

She looked a little stunned. "Dear God. How many women have you been with?"

Now I really don't want to come clean with her. "Maybe we shouldn't talk about this right now. Maybe now is a bad time to be doing this." I did have some intention of trying to get her into bed, after all. Sometime in the near future, even—if things all worked out.

But then she reached out and took my hand again, giving me a reassuring look. "Ashton, you can be honest with me. I won't judge you for anything you tell me."

A part of me wanted to fudge the numbers at least a little. But that purely honest expression she wore would make me feel like a jackass if I lied to her.

So I went for the whole truth and nothing but the truth. "I was a player in high school and college. I never had one single relationship. I stayed away from commitments at all costs. That's why what I felt for Natalia took me by complete surprise. My number is—get ready for it." I closed my eyes, so I wouldn't have to see her reaction and have that etched in my memory bank forever. "Thirty-seven."

The silence had me opening my eyes to look at her. What I found was her smiling face. "Thank you, Ashton."

There wasn't a clue in my mind as to why she would thank me for telling her that number. "Thank you?"

Nodding, she said, "Yes. Thank you. I'm not going to judge you for something that's so natural—and I remember being in high school too. All the hormones raging around, needing an outlet—I found my outlet in volleyball and physical activity. But I know a lot of people—especially males—who found a much more intimate outlet."

"So you're saying you think I was just a normal male then?" I had kind of thought—later on in life, of course—that I was a horn-dog who would stick my cock into any chick that would let me.

"Completely," she assured me. "You were one of the males who wanted to feel it all, not merely your own palm. And may I be so bold as to go even further?"

"Sure." I was dying to know what else she had to add to that bit of information.

She winked at me with a sly grin. "You probably learned a lot from all those women. Each one taught you a little something that you didn't know before. You catalogued all of this information for future use. For a time when it would be just you and one woman for the rest of your life. You wanted knowledge that would keep things spicy in the bedroom for years and years."

I was shocked and amazed. "Come on! You can read my mind, can't you?"

She shook her head as she laughed. "It's just psychology, really." With a slap on my shoulder, she went on, "Young men who become sexual extroverts usually start off just trying to get it into someone, anyone really."

I nodded. "Yep. You're right about that." I had never told a single soul what I was about to tell Nina. "I've never told anyone about my first time."

Her hand flew to her mouth. "God! She was hideous, wasn't she?"

I shook my head. "Nope."

"Very young?" she asked, and now she did wear a judgmental expression.

"Not at all." I had to tell her before she came up with any more bad ideas. "She was my sophomore English teacher."

She gasped, "No!"

"Yes. And I never told a single soul about that." It felt freeing to admit that after all these years. "I found her crying in the parking lot of one of the local grocery stores. I had just gotten my driver's license and was driving the family car to the store to pick up a few things for my mother. I saw Mrs. Kingston with her head on the steering wheel of her car."

Nina looked thoroughly puzzled. "And that got you the invitation to have sex with her?"

"She had just caught her husband with another woman." I leaned in as if it was some big secret and whispered the rest, "She asked me to follow her home after she told me about everything. She told me that all she could think about was getting back at him for what he'd done. And she told me I could help her do that. Only I couldn't ever tell a soul about it."

"That was very wrong of her, Ashton." Nina shook her head as her eyes went big. "So not right."

"Right or wrong, I didn't care. Without even trying, I'd scored my first piece of ass. Once I had that initial sexual act over with, I was ready to move on to better things. Things like picking up my game to score more tail." Suddenly I felt like that little jackass I was back then, and I didn't like it at all. "I was an ass. I know I was. After I met Natalia, all that went away. That attitude disappeared like magic. And it has never returned."

And as I looked at Nina, I was positive that it never would.

CHAPTER NINE

Nina

I woke up early the next morning. Julia had given each couple one meal a day to cook. It was Sunday, and Ashton and I had been assigned breakfast duty.

The night had ended on a great note. He'd confided in me about something he had never told a single person. I thought that was great progress. And the fact that he seemed kind of surprised when I walked him to my door, kissed him on the cheek, then told him good-night was just the icing on the cake.

I could feel him trusting me more and more. And I knew I was falling hard for the man. It was scary how much I thought about him. How much I genuinely cared for him—that was something that was new to me.

His feelings and his state of mind had suddenly become a top priority to me. And I knew I would do whatever I had to for him to feel comfortable at all times with me.

After showering and dressing in some shorts and a T-shirt, I headed to Ashton's room to knock on his door. "Are you up and ready to make breakfast, Ashton?"

He opened the door with a smile on his handsome face. Wearing shorts and a T-shirt too, he and I matched perfectly. "I am. I was just waiting for you to let me know you were ready."

We headed downstairs to the kitchen to see what kinds of supplies were available to us. "Are you a good cook, Ashton?"

His wide shoulders shrugged. "I'm not sure. No one has told me that I am. But then again, I haven't cooked for anyone else in a while, only myself. I like the food I make though."

I found it a little sad that he hadn't cooked for anyone. "At my apartment, we generally only cook when we want to. When we do want to, we cook enough for all of us. I haven't made anything for breakfast in a long time. But breakfast isn't hard to make anyway."

I was singing a different tune as soon as we walked into the gourmet kitchen—I was in over my head and knew it immediately. I spun around in a circle. "Ashton, I don't even know where the fridge is."

"These rich people's houses have appliances configured right into the walls." He found the fridge, which was the same color of the wood-paneled wall, and opened it. "See?"

The next thing that had me befuddled was the range. "And how about that thing? Can you work it? There're so many burners and knobs, it looks like you would need a college degree just to cook on it."

His lips pulled up to one side as he looked it over. "Ah. We'll get the hang of it. Come on, let's decide what we're going to make. We've got eggs." He handed me the carton, and I placed them on the island countertop.

"I wonder if they have stuff for us to make pancakes," I said as I began to push on the wall to see if I could find some hidden cabinets somewhere. I found a pantry full of food. Next to it was another area, where all kinds of fancy cookware and cooking devices were kept. "Holy hell, being rich means you've got everything in the world at your fingertips." I spotted a Belgian waffle maker and grabbed it, taking it back out to the kitchen.

Ashton had taken out milk, cheeses, some cream, and all kinds of jellies and jams. "Oh, a waffle maker. I like waffles better than pancakes. Glad you found that, Nina."

"What I didn't find was waffle mix. But there were all the ingredients in there to make up some batter." I pulled out my cell to look up a recipe. "Flour, sugar, baking powder, you name it, they've got it. Now to find a recipe. For the record, I like waffles better too."

"I'm thinking waffles, scrambled eggs." Ashton reached back in the fridge, pulling out a package of bacon and a tube of breakfast sausage. "Which one, bacon or sausage?"

"Well, to be honest, I can't cook bacon to save my life." I was terrible with the stuff. "I love it, but I always burn the hell out of it."

"I cook it in the oven, and it always comes out perfect." He smiled at me then tossed the sausage to me. "Can you make some sausage patties then?"

"I can do that." I caught the package of breakfast meat and placed it next to the waffle ingredients. "I think two types of meat and two entrees is plenty for us all. Don't you?"

"You bet." He went to the oven, which was built into the wall. After studying it for a moment, he pushed some buttons, and it began to heat up. "Now to find a cookie sheet and a bowl to mix the eggs in."

Jerking my head to the hidden room of cooking utensils, I said, "In there. Everything you could ever need is in that little room off the back of the pantry."

His awe was obvious as he went into the deluxe pantry. "Holy crap!"

"I know, right." I laughed as I thought about how someone who was used to have so many things at their disposal would survive with the few items I had at my apartment.

When he came back, he had a weird looking copper pan with a rack built into it. "You will never guess what I found in there, Nina."

"If you're talking about the thing in your hand, you're right. I couldn't possibly guess what that thing is called or what it's used for." I looked the thing over as he sat it on the countertop.

"Watch this." He took the bacon out of the package, then laid it in strips over the raised rack. "Tada! This will turn out even better than the way I make it at home." He went to the sink to wash his hands, which I noted with appreciation.

A man who knows his way around a kitchen and knows when to wash his hands is my kind of man.

"What do you call that thing?" I wanted to know because I was going to buy him one the next time there was a reason to give presents. If it wasn't out of my price range.

"I don't know," he said as he looked at it. "A bacon rack maybe."

Taking a quick picture of it with my cell, I gave my excuse, "I'll ask social media. Someone out there will know."

Ashton went on to his next task of finding a bowl to mix the eggs in. He came out with three different kinds of syrups. "You can put these out with your waffles."

"Did you see any whipped cream in the fridge?" I found a measuring cup and put some flour in it. "I'd like to have that available for the waffles too. Oh, and fresh fruit too. Was there any of that in there?"

"There were some strawberries. But I didn't see any whipped cream." He looked at the pint of cream he'd put on the countertop. "I can make some sweet cream out of that, though."

He was a good cook. "Can you really?"

With a nod, he smiled. "I can. So, you get those strawberries and cut them up, and I'll make the cream."

"We're a pretty good team, I think." I moved past him to get to the fridge to find him briefly blocking my way while he gave me a peck on the cheek.

"I agree."

All I could do was smile like an idiot as I kept on moving, not wanting our first kiss to be interrupted by the sound of the oven dinging or people coming to eat.

But he had me in a whirlwind of emotions and feelings.

My hands trembled as I took the strawberries out and placed them on the counter. "The knives," I said as I looked around the room.

Ashton turned around then came right toward me. He stopped

right in front of me, putting one hand around me. Our faces were so close, I could feel his warm breath on my lips. Then he brought his hand back with a small knife in it. "Here ya go."

As quick as he came to me, he was gone. And I was breathless and damp in some very interesting places.

I tried to think of some way I could return the favor. I spied an outlet near him where I could plug in the waffle maker. Picking it up, I walked over to the outlet. The oven dinged. Ashton grabbed the rack of bacon and walked away.

Quickly, I abandoned that idea, plugging the waffle maker in where it made more sense. Near where I was working.

"Did you happen to see a mixer when you were back there?" he asked me as he walked toward the pantry.

"The only one I saw was that huge red thing that had its own table back there." I tried to think of the name I'd seen on it. "The Kitchen something or other."

"Oh, yeah," he called out. "I see it. Damn, that's going to be a bitch to clean."

"Not to worry, Ashton. We won't be the ones cleaning up. Their maid will."

He popped his head out to look at me. "No way. We get to cook, and there's no cleaning involved?" He looked positively stoked. "What a win for us! I'd cook way more often and try a lot of different things if I didn't have to clean up afterward."

A little smile moved over my lips. I could just imagine us in the future, him doing the cooking, me doing the cleaning. An even trade that he and I could both live with, if we were ever able to move things further. "I don't mind cleaning. It's the cooking that's the real chore to me. I actually find it relaxing to wash dishes in hot soapy water."

"Shut up!" He looked at me as if he couldn't believe what he'd heard. "I swear you can read my mind. Come clean with me already, Nina. This is too much."

"Don't be silly. I know you're exaggerating." I pulled open a drawer and found a wire whisk. "Here, you can use this to stir those eggs." I tossed it to him.

He caught it and winked at me. "We really do make a great team, don't we?"

"I think so." With a skip in my step, I thought everything was going so well. I headed to the pantry to get some cooking spray and tripped over my own feet. "Shit!" I was headed to the floor, face first.

A pair of strong hands grabbed me by the waist. "Whoa." Ashton pulled me back up as he chuckled with his deep voice. "Getting a little tangled up in yourself there, aren't ya?"

I couldn't take in any air. His hands on my waist, his body right behind mine, it was all too much. My senses were on overload. My mouth began to water, my lips tingled. This was it.

He was going to turn me in his arms, and we were going to have our first kiss.

I just knew it!

His lips brushed against my neck. "Nina ..."

Laughter came trickling into the kitchen. The others were up and just about to walk in.

Well, damn!

CHAPTER TEN

Ashton

I was going to kiss her. I had her in my arms; my lips were on her neck. And then they showed up.

Never in my life had I been so disappointed to see my friends.

And with their arrival, and their eyes on us, our great teamwork in the kitchen came to an end. It was a fiasco with them watching us. I dropped the eggs, Nina overfilled the waffle maker, making a huge mess on the countertop that Julia told us not to worry about.

All I really wanted was for them to leave us alone.

And as we placed the burnt bacon, the chewy waffles, and the unsweetened cream that tasted like crap on the buffet table, I knew Nina could be the one for me.

Well, the other one for me.

I had found true love once, and now it seemed I was being offered a second chance.

As we sat at the breakfast table, barely eating the meal we'd had such great hopes for until it all went awry, Nina took all the ridicule right along with me. "Yeah, yeah," she said to them all. "It was going well until you four showed up. That's all I can tell you. Right, Ashton?"

With a nod, I agreed. "It was going well." I cut my eyes to look at Nina, who was suddenly blushing.

I knew she was remembering the near-kiss we'd almost shared. I knew she would've kissed me right back. There was a tablecloth hiding us from the waist down, so I moved my hand over her knee and felt goosebumps pepper her satin-smooth skin. It made my dick hard, simply touching her like that.

Nina made me feel like a whole man again. I'd lost that man. But she had found him, somehow.

I had no idea how she had managed to punch through all the armor that surrounded my heart to set it free again, but she had. And I was ready to let it all down.

Artimus had planned out all of our time for our last day. "We've got shopping at the local markets next on our itinerary. And don't even think about saying you don't have any extra money to spend."

Nina was quick to say, "I really don't, Artimus. I can just stay here while you guys go. Or I can go and just window shop, I guess. I don't really like window shopping, though. It's like, when I have money, I can't find anything I want. When I don't have any, I find so much that I want."

"I'll stay here with her. I don't need anything, and I hate to buy things I don't need." I was just making any excuse I could to get to be alone with her again.

Julia had brought a bag with her, and it was near her feet under the table. "We've gotten you all some little gifts to say thank you for being our guests for the weekend." She put a small pink bag in front of the ladies and small black bags in front of Duke and myself. "Go ahead. See what we've given you guys. You know you're our very best friends in the whole world."

Lila whined, "I feel bad now, you guys. We didn't give you anything. We would've brought wine and a cheeseboard, but you have much better wine than we could buy anyway."

"And cheese," Duke added.

Artimus stepped in. "Don't even think about that. You gave us the pleasure of your company for the entire weekend. You could've done anything you wanted to, and you chose to spend it with us. Now enjoy what we've given you and stop making a fuss."

Nina nudged me in the ribs with her elbow. "Thank you, guys. This is an unexpected and very nice surprise."

"Yeah, thanks, Artimus, Julia." I gave them my thanks, with Nina's urging, even though I didn't think they needed to give us anything. "Just being your friend is enough for me, but the present is appreciated."

Lila peeked into her bag. "What's in here?"

Duke reached into his bag then pulled out a bottle of 80-year-old scotch. "Whoa!"

"Keep digging," Artimus coached him.

I watched as Nina and Lila each pulled out bottles of rare and very expensive bottles of wine. And when I pulled out the largest gift of mine, I found the most expensive bourbon money could buy.

The girls got some jewelry; Lila, emeralds, Nina, sapphires. Duke and I got watches. And at the very bottom of the bag were prepaid Visa cards. The holders they came in told us there was 5000 dollars on each card.

"Shut up!" I shouted as I stood up.

I didn't bother holding back; I went to Artimus and hugged him, then picked Julia up and swung her around as she yelped, "Ashton Lange!"

Everyone followed suit, hugging and thanking our hosts for everything, including the fun-filled weekend. And we all told them how they didn't have to do that every time we came for a visit.

So, with money in hand, how could we not go along with our hosts to the markets?

That meant that alone time with Nina would have to wait once again, and that I'd have to keep my hands more or less to myself. It didn't feel right to make any move, other than holding her hand as we walked around the shops.

Her hand moved over a gorgeous silk wrap. There were blues and greens woven through it, and it would look great on her. She pulled up the price tag. "Oh, no." She quickly put it back.

I picked it up to see what the issue was. She'd just gotten a nice little bit cash, after all. "Nina. It's just five hundred dollars. You can afford that."

"No way!" She looked at me as if I was nuts. "Are you crazy? That's way too much for anything like that."

The way the saleslady looked at her made me cringe. We were shopping in the Hamptons. People around this place didn't balk at prices if the item was worth it.

The woman waddled up to us, her nose turned up. "I can assure you that the wrap you're looking at is an item that you could use with many other articles of clothing. It could work with everything, from adding a little splash to a black cocktail dress, to wearing it around your waist when you're in a bikini. It serves many purposes and would add to your wardrobe, I can assure you."

Nina looked at me over her shoulder. "Something this pricey wouldn't quite match the rest of my wardrobe. Thank you, though."

Nina walked away, and I leaned in to whispered to the saleslady. "Put it on hold, and I'll be back for it in a little while."

With a smile, she took it off the rack. "Thank you, sir."

With a nod, I left to catch up to Nina, who had already made it to the next shop. I bumped her shoulder with mine. "You know, if your wardrobe needs some punching up, now is the time to do that. You've got more than enough money to do that right now."

She looked around. "These prices are all outrageous."

I had to agree, but she needed to get some things for herself. She deserved to treat herself. "Okay, how about the main things a woman needs in her closet?"

"Like?" she asked, with a shake of her head.

"You tell me. I'm not a woman."

Tapping her chin, she thought about it. "I like to have a good pair of boots for the winter. Those things can be very expensive if you want good quality that will last."

"And what about that little black dress that lady back there talked about?" I reminded her. "An expensive one would see you through many years. And each time you wore it, you could change up the look with an accent piece." I knew I was making progress when her head started swiveling around.

"Yes, you're right about that." She went to a rack of stylish dresses and began looking through them. But then her eyes went to me. "And what about you? What are some things that you need and haven't bought for yourself in a while?"

Shoving my hands into my pockets, I had no idea where to start. "My apartment could use some homey touches."

That was no joke. I had one sofa. I had bought that brand new, though. It was nice, a dark leather piece. My windows had miniblinds on them, but I had never bought curtains to make it look homey.

My apartment wasn't my sanctuary. It was the place I lived, and that was about it.

It was in a nice building. And the small two-bedroom, one bath, was very nice. All hardwood floors, tile in the kitchen and bathroom, granite countertops throughout the kitchen and bathroom, all the bells and whistles. But it didn't feel like home. Mostly because I hadn't ever made it into a real home.

Natalia would've made it a home.

I shook my head to clear it. I couldn't be thinking about that. My life was changing, moving forward.

Julia and Lila showed up with their husbands, and the girls went crazy over all the clothing. We men were put on the back burner, and Artimus told them that we would be doing some shopping on our own. All they needed to do was give him a call, and we would meet back up.

I left with my friends and found Artimus taking us to a small Irish pub to grab a drink. We all sat at a small round table in the dimly lit place, which smelled of dark beer and salty bread. "Did this weekend earn you Nina's favor, Ashton?" Artimus asked me with what I could only guess was his attempt at an Irish accent.

Duke jabbed me in the ribs with his elbow, joining Artimus in the running for the world's worst Irish accent. "Did you get her where ya wanted her?"

"This weekend wasn't exactly about getting her into bed. I think more of her than that." I took the beer the waiter handed to me and took a drink of it. It was a stout beer, with lots of hops and barley. The foam was thick and creamy, and I took another drink. "This is good."

Duke raised his mug, and so did Artimus. "Here's to you and Nina. It's about time."

I clinked my mug to theirs before we all took a drink.

It *was* about time. I knew that. I had lived far too long in this limbo-like state.

Sure, I hadn't fallen behind in my career. I hadn't become some drunk who couldn't function. But I had lost myself when I lost Natalia. And now I was ready for what lay ahead of me.

A future with Nina.

And I could tell she wanted that too. She wasn't playing with me. She was laying down the brickwork to make sure we would have a solid foundation to build on.

"How did I get so lucky to have a woman like Nina Kramer care about me?" I asked my friends.

Duke, always the joker, said, "No one knows for sure, you old dog. Just be thankful, and don't drag your feet much longer. Hell, you've already made the girl wait two years for you."

He was right, on all fronts. And just as I was about to make another toast, the bartender turned up the television and the broadcast took my attention as the reporter on screen gave us the date and the local weather.

Duke and Artimus looked only at me as I watched the television. "I forgot what day it is." I looked back at them. "Today's the anniversary of Natalia's death. I have lived for this day each and every year since she died. And now I've forgotten it. Nina made me forget about her. I promised I'd never forget about her."

I can't let this happen.

CHAPTER ELEVEN

Nina

One solid week passed without me seeing Ashton at all. It was as if he'd turned into a ghost at the station. His work got done, but no one saw him doing it.

The ride home that Sunday evening after our wonderful weekend was a quiet one. Ashton claimed he was just tired and that was why he was being so quiet. He had the driver drop him off first, leaving me with Lila and Duke.

When I asked Duke if Ashton had said anything to him about being upset about something, he told me there was nothing. So, I took Ashton at his word, thinking he was really tired.

Monday came, and I fully expected to see Ashton all chipper after a good night's rest. But I never saw him at all. And the door to his office was closed and locked. I knew that because I tried to open it.

I let it go that first day, thinking that maybe he was sick. Then Tuesday came, and the same thing happened, door closed and locked, Ashton nowhere to be seen by anyone.

At the daily coffee breaks with Lila and Julia, I asked them both to see what they could find out about the suddenly elusive man.

I'd thought we were headed in the right direction. He had almost kissed me, after all. His actions now made no sense to me.

The only information that I got was from Julia, telling me that he was actually at the station. He was doing his work from his office and watching the newscasts from there too, directing the cameramen through an earpiece from his desk.

I wondered what he was doing for lunch all those days. Lila told me she saw food being delivered a couple of times. He was eating in his office as well.

It wasn't like Ashton Lange to keep to himself the way he was doing. He was a social person. And I was getting worried about the man.

If he'd changed his mind about us, all he would've had to do was tell me that. I would understand. It would hurt, but I would get it.

I didn't get what he was doing by becoming a recluse right there at work. If he wasn't socializing at work or home, then when was he talking to people?

I headed up to see Artimus and Duke, hoping to get some answers. I had a feeling they were being tight-lipped with their wives about Ashton's behavior. Maybe their wives weren't being as demanding as I could be.

Heading up to their offices on the top floor, I got off the elevator and saw Brady, the receptionist, working with his intern, Veronica. She was the newest addition to our coffee meetings, but she'd missed it that morning. Brady had her busy elsewhere, but where exactly that was, none of us knew. When I'd asked that morning, he'd simply said that she was indisposed at the moment and wouldn't be joining us for coffee.

As Brady was busily cleaning the chairs in the lobby, I took a moment to talk to Veronica. Leaning on the desk she was dusting, I asked, "So, what were you up to that you couldn't have coffee with us this morning, Veronica?"

When her cheeks blushed immediately, I had my answer. Not that she gave much away, but I'd already had my suspicions. "Oh, I had to clean out the closet with the office supplies in it. It took me most of the morning."

Looking over my shoulder at Brady's back, I smiled as I saw the way he'd gone stiff. He and she had a thing going on. We all knew it, even though they tried to pretend their relationship was completely professional.

"Is that so?" I asked. "You know, we have an excellent maintenance and janitorial staff that takes care of things like that. Don't let the boss-man make you do unnecessary chores."

Suddenly Brady was right behind me. "I'm training her to be the best receptionist there is. Merely standing at a desk looking pretty won't cut it in this busy." He pointed at Artimus' office. "He and Duke are waiting for you, since you called this impromptu meeting. You should hurry. They don't have all the time in the world, you know."

Veronica turned away to get busy with something else. "See you later, Nina."

"Yeah, later." I walked to the door to Artimus' office and gave a quick knock. "It's Nina."

The door opened, Artimus using the button under his desk so neither of them would have to get up. I found Duke and him talking away about the football game that'd been on the night before. "And the yardage he made was impressive too," Duke said, before they turned their attention to me. "Hey, Nina. What's up?"

"I've got questions." I took a seat in front of the desk, next to the one Duke occupied.

Artimus steepled his fingers as he sat in his chair behind the desk. "Shoot."

"I want to know what the hell is wrong with Ashton. And I know you two know what it is." I leaned forward, placing my palms on the desk. "And I'm not leaving here without an answer. So, fess up, guys."

I watched the men as they eyed each other, then Duke looked at me. "Nina, we have to be respectful of our friend. We're not about to be telling tales he's asked us to keep quiet about. Not even to you."

Now I knew for sure that they knew what was going on. "Did he tell you not to tell me?"

Artimus shook his head. "He didn't have to. We know Ashton pretty well by now. If he wanted you to know, he would've told you about it himself. And the fact that he's virtually gone into hiding says he doesn't want to talk about this with anyone. Not even us. And we won't push him to do something he doesn't want to do."

They were good friends; I had to admit that. But they weren't thinking things through. "This isn't healthy for Ashton, you guys. Being all alone, all the time, isn't good for a person. And leaving your friend alone, just because he thinks that's what he wants, is okay, but only for a short amount of time. It's Friday. It's been an entire week. That man has come in early every day to get into his office before anyone can see him. He leaves later than everyone else for the same reason."

Duke shrugged. "Maybe it was the black eye at first."

Artimus frowned at him. "Whatever it was, if he wanted anyone to know, he would've said something. He hasn't said a thing, so neither should we."

Man, these guys are tight-lipped!

"While I'm stoked to see you two are truly Ashton's friends, if you really want to help him then you've got to do something to get him out of this funk he's in. Look, if he's second-guessing whatever happened between me and him last weekend, I can understand that. I've never pushed him, and I never will. He deserves to know that, doesn't he?"

Duke nodded. "Yeah."

"I just need him to get out of his office for even a few minutes. If I see him, then I know he'll talk to me, and we can set things straight." Looking at Artimus, I implored him, "Can't you get him out of that office for some reason today?"

With a deep sigh, Artimus nodded. "Yes, I think I can. I'll ask him to come up to see me. Give me a half hour. You'll have two chances to see him then. One when he's coming up and one when he's going back down. That's about all I can do for you, Nina."

With a nod, I had what I wanted and got up to leave. "Thank you. Once we talk, he'll come out of this funk. You'll see."

I went down to my office and waited to catch Ashton walking down the hallway, right past my open door. There was no other way to get to the elevator.

Pretending to be typing away on my laptop, I made sure to keep my eyes locked on the hallway. And sure enough, Ashton walked by. And he walked by so quickly, not even turning his head the slightest bit in my direction, that it shocked me.

My chance had come, and I bolted out of my chair. As soon as I was in the hallway, I shouted out after him, "Ashton!"

He stopped, his body stiff, but he didn't turn around. "I'm in a hurry." He began walking again, as if that would be enough to stop me.

He was wrong. I hurried to catch up to him before he could get on that elevator. "Ashton, just wait a minute." I got close enough to put my hand on his shoulder. "Please."

Stopping once again, he didn't turn around to look at me. "What?"

I got in front of him, so he didn't have any choice but to look at me. "What the hell have you been doing all week?"

"Working." He cut his eyes to the side, avoiding me still.

"You've never worked this way before. So why are you being so reclusive now?" I asked him, and then put my hand on his chin to force his face to mine. His eye was no longer black. There was no evidence of the injury he'd sustained from the volleyball accident at all. "Your eye looks like it's back to normal. You look like yourself again. Handsome as ever. Come on, Ashton. Just be honest with me. What's wrong?"

When he finally looked into my eyes, my heart froze. There was so much sadness behind them. It tore at my heart to see that sadness again. "You wouldn't understand."

"Try me."

He shook his head. "I don't want to."

I was perplexed. I had no idea what the hell to say to the man. But I came up with something. "Please." It was all I could think to do. Appeal to his caring nature. At least the one he used to have.

With another shake of his head he tried to walk around me. "I've got to go."

"To your meeting with Artimus?" I asked as I caught him by the arm to stop him.

Now his eyes narrowed at me. "How do you know about that?"

"Because I asked him to get you out of your office, so I would have a chance to see you. To talk to you. So there's no need to rush. He won't be freaking out when you don't come up to see him. He'll know I got to you." I smiled at him to let him know I wasn't going to be a bitch about whatever rejection I was sure would be coming my way. "Come on; we need to talk. I won't be mad about anything you have to say to me. Even if it's something I don't want to hear. I promise."

The way his face turned red told me he was less than pleased about my little plan with Artimus. "What the hell, Nina? You went behind my back—bothered my friends, not to mention my boss, and for what? I have my own reasons for staying in my office."

"And they are?" I asked.

He jerked his arm out of my hand then headed back to his office. "To stay away from you!"

Stunned, I stood there, watching him storm away from me.

What did I do to deserve that?

12

CHAPTER TWELVE

Artimus

Seeing her only made things worse. The scent of her honeysuckle shampoo still lingered in my nose. Nina had a way of consuming my every thought, no matter how hard I tried not to let her do that to me.

I closed and locked my office door behind me. Then I pulled out my cell and tapped in a text to Artimus, letting him know that it wasn't cool, what he and Nina had tried to pull.

Tossing the phone onto my desk, I went to lie on the sofa next to the window. Staring out at the clouds above the city, rather than at the busy streets below, I tried to forget about Nina.

The woman had plagued my dreams since the night I got back home. Every time I closed my eyes, there she was. Most people wouldn't think that would be such a bad thing.

It was bad to me. Because Nina had knocked Natalia right out of my mind. No dreams of Natalia came at all. I'd lived with those dreams—which more often than not turned into nightmares—for four years. How had she suddenly made them all go away?

How had Nina embedded herself into my brain so much that I'd forgotten the anniversary of Natalia's death?

It wasn't right.

I couldn't just go on and forget about the woman I'd loved. The woman I had planned to marry—to make a family with and spend my whole life with.

But Nina had come along and so easily pushed Natalia all the way out. And I couldn't allow that to happen.

It wouldn't be fair to Natalia.

Closing my eyes, I felt the familiar feeling of exhaustion creeping up on me. I wouldn't let myself sleep that much. Not when every one of my dreams this last week had been erotic—and Nina the star of them all.

The guilt I felt was overwhelming. I was a wreck. A shell of the man I had managed to become after my fiancée's death. And there was no one to blame for that but Nina.

As I lay there, berating myself for forgetting Natalia, I thought about Artimus and Duke.

They must've kept what happened to themselves. If they'd told Nina, then she would have led with that.

I knew it wasn't Nina's fault that I had let Natalia slip out of my head. But I did know that if I kept seeing Nina, then I would lose Natalia completely. And I didn't want that.

My head ached with yet another headache. I had gotten one or two each day since the weekend had ended. Pulling the bottle of pills out of my pocket, I sat up and popped a couple into my mouth, swallowing them down.

Lying back on the sofa, I let the ibuprofen work on my aching head. With my eyes closed, it didn't take long at all for sleep to take me. And then the dream began.

I went to Nina's apartment, finding her there alone, her roommates out for the night. She wiggled her finger at me, beckoning me to her bedroom. "Follow me, Ashton."

"Right behind you, baby." I followed her like a lamb to the slaughter, unafraid, and without remorse.

My hands settled on round hips that were covered in dark green silk. She had on a skimpy nightgown that I couldn't wait to rid her of. After I kicked the door shut, Nina turned around to face me.

The smile on her face told me she had something in mind. Her hands moved to my chest, stopping me from moving forward. She moved them down my body slowly, going to her knees in front of me.

Licking her lips, she undid my jeans, then released my cock. Her soft hands moved up and down me as she kissed the tip. My entire body shuddered with desire. I ran my hands through her hair. "Oh, baby."

Her lips flowed over the head of my erect cock a few times as her hands stroked the shaft. Giving her head a little push had her mouth opening wide as she took me all the way in. She moaned with pleasure, her tongue running up the underside of my cock as she sucked gently.

I had to lean back on the door to steady myself as she sucked me off. Watching her as her head moved up and down with her long even strokes, I saw her in a glowing light.

Her mouth felt so hot, it seemed impossible. And all I could think about was how it would feel to finally put my cock into an even hotter place on her gorgeous body. My cock jerked as my cum spurted down her throat.

She drank it up then looked up at me, a bit of my seed dangling from her lower lip before she licked it off. I pulled her up, then stepped out of jeans that had fallen to my ankles. Her hands moved under my T-shirt, lifting it off me.

I took the hem of her gown and pulled it off over her head, leaving her gloriously naked in front of me. Her tits were huge, the nipples hard as rocks. Pushing her back onto the bed, I moved my body over hers, straddling her.

Playing with her nipples, I watched them grow even harder. "Shit, you're beautiful, Nina."

She didn't say a word back to me, but her hands moved to cover both of mine as she helped me massage her big, juicy tits. I leaned over and took one taut nipple into my mouth.

Once I sank my teeth into it, she let out a growl. "Suck it."

I sucked on her swollen nipple as I squeezed her other tit. All the while, she moaned and bucked underneath me. All the wiggling she did was making me lose focus. I pinned her shoulders to the bed, holding her still so I could continue biting and sucking her sweet tit.

She whined a bit, then screamed as she arched up to me. "I'm coming!"

I moved quickly, pushing her legs apart so I could stick my hard and aching cock into her pulsing pussy. She wrapped her legs around me, holding me tight. It was obvious that she didn't want me to pull out of her for even a second as she screamed my name over and over.

Her nails dug into my back as her body was racked with pleasure. Her cunt was tight around my cock, and the way it convulsed as her juices flowed freely had me fucking her hard and fast.

Pounding her hot cunt with a ruthlessness that defied imagination, I took Nina exactly the way I wanted to. With unadulterated passion.

I owned her body. No one could ever make her feel the way I could.

"Open your eyes, baby," I ordered her. I wanted to stare into those green depths as I made her mine.

She held tightly to my shoulders as she opened her eyes and stared into mine. I could see her giving it all to me. Her body, her heart, her soul. It was all mine now. I had earned her love, her worship.

And as I looked into her eyes, my body began to shake. It was all too real. She was under me; I was inside of her. And only then did I realize that I didn't own her. She owned me.

And I gave myself to her without her ever asking me to. "I'm yours, Nina."

With one nod of her pretty head, she had me. "I know, baby. Now take me in the ass."

With a smile, I pulled out of her then turned her onto her stomach. I kept her body flat on the bed, took one of her hands and pulled it up above her head as I slid my body over hers until my cock was on the cusp of her asshole.

She pushed her ass up, and I used my fingertip to prepare her before plunging inside of her even tighter hole. With a gasp from her, I put my lips on the side of her neck. "Hush. It'll be okay." I kissed her neck as I fucked her in the ass. Her whimpers became moans, and she moved with me to get my dick into her as deep as it would go.

Grinding hard against her ass, I didn't stop until she was crying out her pleasure. "I'm coming again!"

I let her body climax then pulled out of her. Turning her over, I spread her legs apart as her body shook with the strong orgasm. Juices poured from her cunt, and I ran my tongue over her before pushing into her pussy to eat her. I played with her clit to get her to keep producing the sweet nectar she gave me.

My cock was straining with the need to release, so I kissed my way up her body, then shoved my cock into her. With hard, demanding thrusts, I finally found my end, filling her with my hot seed.

We both groaned as I shot my load into her. Her hands moved through my hair as she whispered in my ear. "I want your baby, Ashton. I want us to be a family. Give it to me."

I bit her neck, making her scream with delight. "I'll give it to you, Nina. I won't stop until your belly is round with my baby." I began to move against her again as my cock got hard once more. "I'll fuck you all night long and into the next day."

Her breathing was ragged as she said in a quiet voice, "Please, Ashton, please fuck me all night long. I need you inside of me."

"You're damn right, you do." I kissed her sweet lips and off we went again into the bliss of the best sex either of us had ever had.

The sound of my phone beeping had my eyes springing open. It took me a few minutes to pull myself completely out of sleep and the dream I'd been in.

"Shit!"

I sat up, holding my head in my hands. The dream had felt so real; my cock was at full attention. I had to give myself a minute for it to go back to a normal state before I stood up.

Taking a deep breath, I finally got up and went to my desk to see who had texted me. Artimus had sent me a message.

-I wouldn't be a good friend if I let this go on and did nothing about it. This therapist comes highly recommended. You need to set up an appointment with Jasmine Patel. I've sent you an email with a link to her website. Read the reviews and her mission. I think you'll like what you see, Ashton. Enough is enough. Stop missing out on a future because you're stuck in the past.-

I fell into my chair and stared at the message. No one had any idea how I felt. No one knew the guilt I was plagued with. No one could ever understand what it meant to be a man who'd killed the woman he loved.

I didn't need a therapist. I needed to get Nina out of my head so that Natalia could come back.

I knew any therapist would think that the only way I could live a normal life would be to put Natalia out of my mind.

Only I didn't want to lose my fiancée.

I've got to do what's right for me, not what others think is best. And that's that.

CHAPTER THIRTEEN

Nina

The nerve of that man!

Ashton Lange marched away from me as if he was pissed.

At me!

I hadn't done one damn thing wrong to that man, and there he was hiding from me as if I was some banshee bitch that was harassing his ass or something. If he thought I was going to take what he'd said lying down, he had another think coming.

I was the one who ended up getting on that elevator instead of him, and I went up to vent my anger and frustration to my friends.

Julia saw the heat in my eyes as I came into her office. "I cannot believe this, Julia." I flopped down on one of the sofas in her office. "Ashton has been hiding in his office to stay away from me. From me!"

My entire body was shaking. Julia went to the mini fridge and pulled out a bottle of wine. "This looks like a job for some wine." She poured me a glass, then one for herself just as Lila knocked on the door. Julia went to the door to open it. "She's fit to be tied, Lila. Ashton has really done it this time."

Lila jerked her head toward the wine glasses. "Pour me one while you're at it. I know this will put my panties in a wad too." She made her way to me, taking a seat right next to me as she took my hand in hers. "Tell us all about it, Nina."

"H ... he ... he," I took a deep breath in an attempt to pull myself together. "He told me he's been staying in his office to stay away from me." And then the tears exploded. "What did I do wrong?"

Lila patted my hand. "Nothing. Not one damn thing, Nina."

Julia placed one of the glasses in my hand. "Here, drink this. It'll calm you down so you can vent more therapeutically."

I had half the glass in my gut before Lila peeled it away from me. "Too fast. You don't need to get hammered, just chilled out a bit."

Nodding, I knew she was right. If I did get drunk, I wouldn't be able to control myself. I would end up banging on Ashton's door, demanding to be let in so I could belt him one right in the kisser.

Julia took a seat on the sofa across from us. "I wonder why he would want to avoid you. You two had a good time last weekend, didn't you? Was there something that happened between you two that you've left out of our conversations? Be honest."

I thought about it. Had I not paid attention to something that had upset Ashton? "I can't think of anything that could've led to him acting this way." I hadn't told them one thing—it hadn't seemed right to tell anyone about what had almost happened. "When he and I were making breakfast, right before you guys came into the kitchen, he and I almost kissed."

Lila shook her head as she looked confused. "Why didn't you tell us this before?"

With a shrug, I answered, "I don't know. It seemed like a small thing. And it didn't happen. He never kissed me. So, why bother telling anyone about it?"

Julia sighed. "I don't know. I guess you were right not to mention it to us. But that still doesn't help us make sense of things. If he was about to kiss you then, then what the hell could be going on in that man's head right now?"

"That weekend was supposed to draw you guys closer together, not pull you further apart," Lila said then took a drink of the wine. "That man is so confusing."

Julia quirked her lips to one side, looking deep in thought. "You know, if the problem in the first place was this business with his fiancée, then do you think this could have something to do with her again?"

I nodded, then jumped up, stomping my feet as I hopped up and down in a fit. "Of course she has something to do with this! Be he was being so good with talking to me about her. So why is this happening now?"

There was no way that I could take any more of this. It was making me crazy.

Lila grabbed me, placing my ass back on the sofa. "Take a sip, Nina." She held the wine glass to my lips.

I took a sip, but it didn't do me any good. "I can't do this anymore."

Both of them looked at me with stunned expressions. Lila's mouth gaped open. "You're done with Ashton Lange? After two years, you are really done?"

Nodding, I took another sip. "I can't compete with a dead woman. I never stood a chance. I'm finally getting that through my thick skull. He was never free; I can see that now. She's got a hold on him from the grave. She'll never let go."

Julia was quick to say, "It's not like that, Nina. She's not the one who's holding onto anyone. It's him. He's holding onto her because of the guilt he feels about her death. And he misses her too. Everything between them is unresolved. She left this Earth when they both loved each other so much. They had a whole life planned together. All that went away in a flash."

"And I get that." My hands fisted in my lap. "But I can't keep on trying when he's being mean to me. Ashton has never been mean to me. I don't know how to take it. It just makes me want to get away from him," I took a deep breath, trying to get my thoughts in some semblance of order. "I feel like I don't even know him anymore. How can he act like this after we just had a wonderful, fun weekend of finally getting to really know one another? I just don't understand."

Artimus came through the door that connected his and Julia's offices. "I can hear the shouting all the way in my office. What the hell has happened now, Nina?"

"Ashton told me that I'm the reason he's been hiding in his office. I'm the reason he's been avoiding everyone and everything. And I'm pretty upset—and I'm also done with that man!" I downed the rest of my wine. "Can I leave early and have the rest of the day off? I don't think I can focus on holding those cue cards without throwing them up in the air and yelling at Ashton, since I know he'll be watching from his office."

Julia nodded. "Of course you can."

Artimus looked pissed. "That's it! I'm not going to let my friend throw his life away any longer." He stormed out of the office and back into his.

Julia watched her husband leave. "I wonder what he's got up his sleeve."

"It doesn't matter," I said as I got up to leave. "I'm done. I really am. This is it for me. No matter what Artimus does to get that man to come around, it won't be enough. If it's so easy for him to treat me this way, then I'm done wasting my time waiting around for him."

"You can't stop trying now, Nina," Julie tried. "I believe this is just Ashton's last-ditch effort to keep things the way they are—to keep his fiancée alive in his mind. This is the biggest change we've seen in him in two years—clearly something is happening with him that he hadn't allowed before. He needs help with this. And you seem to be the only one he'll talk to."

"You know what? It's not my responsibility to fix all of him problems. I've tried to help him with that, and where did it get me? If this is the way he responds to someone giving a shit about him, then he can kiss my ass, as far as I'm concerned." I grabbed the doorknob and pulled the door opened. "I'll be at home. I don't know what I'll be doing, but I'll be doing something, I can tell you that much. I will not sit around, hoping that one day Ashton Lange will get his house in order. Because that day will never come."

Lila and Julia came to the door, both enveloping me in a

comforting hug. Julia patted me on the back. "Nina, let things calm down. You're mad right now. And you've got every right to be. But don't do anything that you'll regret."

Lila looked at me with a smile as she winked. "That means don't go finding another man to get under, just so you can get over Ashton."

"I hadn't even thought of that." The idea didn't seem half bad to me. "And just why shouldn't I do that, Lila? It sounds like a great idea."

Her arm went around my shoulders as we all three walked toward the elevator. "Because right now you're mad and hurt. When your judgement is clouded by that, it's never a good time to get under anyone."

Maybe she was right, but maybe she wasn't. All I knew was that I'd wasted the last two years of my life pining after a man who would never accept a future with me, and it was time for a change. No more waiting around for anyone.

Getting onto the elevator, I waved goodbye to my friends as the doors closed. "See you on Monday."

"Have a good weekend," Lila said.

"Be good," Julia threw in just before the doors closed.

The ride down to my floor had me thinking about what they'd said. Why should I be good?

I had been good for years, and where had that gotten me?

Nowhere, that's where.

I went to my office to get my purse and shut down my computer. As I stopped at my door, I looked down the hallway at Ashton's closed one.

He had never closed his door before. There were always people stopping by his office, and he always had a smile for them. Now he wasn't talking to anyone.

As I thought about that, I waited to feel my heart aching for him. But it didn't ache at all. I was that pissed at him.

So, I headed into my office. It seemed I was officially done with Ashton Lange. He'd stepped over a line that I hadn't even known was there. Apparently, having someone turn away from me after I'd given them nothing but compassion and friendship—a bit more than friendship, even—was enough to give me an extreme change of heart.

I wanted him to know how mad I was at him. So, I sat down and wrote him an email that let him know exactly how done I was with him, and why.

Ashton,

I know you've suffered. I was there for you. I never pushed you to do anything you didn't want to. I was your friend.

I'm not sure how things got to be the way they are, but I'm done trying to figure things out.

Here it is in black and white for you: I'm done.

You don't have to hide in your office anymore. I won't be trying to speak with you. I don't even care to be your friend anymore, much less anything more than that.

I'd had this idea that you and I could be something special. I felt it all weekend long too. I had never felt closer to anyone than I felt with you.

Did I make that up?

Was any of it real for you?

Maybe I was living in a fantasy world, to believe that you and I could be more than friends. But that bubble has burst. You blew it all up.

I sat there, reading each word over and over until my eyes grew blurry. Then, one letter at a time, I deleted the whole thing until the page was blank.

No matter what Ashton had done, I wasn't going to hurt him. Not on purpose, I wouldn't.

He had his demons. I was well aware of that fact.

And I wouldn't add to the beating he was already giving himself. But I also wasn't about to keep on trying, to keep on waiting.

That wasn't getting me anywhere, anyway.

CHAPTER FOURTEEN

Ashton

The longer I sat there, looking at the text Artimus had sent to me, the madder I got.

Who did he think he was, sending me that information? Why did he think he could butt into that part of my life?

I had to make some drastic changes, and there was no better time than the present.

Storming up to Artimus' office, I flew off the elevator as Brady and his intern Veronica looked at me with mouths gaping.

"Is Artimus in?" I asked with a sharp tone.

Brady nodded. "Yeah. Are you okay, Ashton?"

"Never better." I hit the door to my boss's office with my fist. "It's me, Artimus. Open up."

Once the door opened, I saw Artimus sitting behind his large desk, looking at me with an alarmed expression. "What the hell, Ashton?"

Taking long strides, I got to his desk where I pounded my fist on top of it. "Who do you think you are?"

His eyes narrowed as he looked at me. "Take a seat."

"No." I banged the desk again. "Why do you think you can butt into my personal business?"

He stood up too, trying to exert his authority, I assumed. "Listen to me, Ashton Lange. I know you're upset and not yourself right now. And I do understand why. But you can't stand here and ask me why I think I have a right to do anything where you're concerned. You are one of my best friends. I can help you—or try to, at least—if I feel you need help. Which you do, by the way."

I hated the fact that he thought I needed help. "You don't understand at all, Artimus. No one does."

"And that's where you're completely wrong, Ashton." He came around his desk to put his hand on my shoulder. "Other people have gone through loss. Other people have lived through the same thing you have. There are people who can help you."

All I could do was shake my head, knowing that he didn't understand what I needed at all. "No one has gone through exactly what I have. No one, Artimus. You could never understand. And I don't expect you to. What I do expect from you is loyalty. But you've just proven to me that your loyalty doesn't lie with me, it lies with Nina. I never expected that from you or Duke."

A wry smile curled his lips. "Have I disappointed you, Ashton?"

With a nod, I answered his question. "More than you know. Being ambushed by the one person I didn't want to see and finding out that it was all your doing—well, that fucking sucks."

"You needed to see her. You needed to talk to her. But I know that didn't go the way I hoped it would." He walked away from me, going to the bar in the far corner of his office and pulling out a bottle of Scotch. "Come, let's have a drink and talk about things."

I didn't want a drink. I just wanted to get shit straight with him and get the hell out of there. But my feet went toward him anyway. My hand took the glass of alcohol. Then my lips parted to drink some of it down.

My body has become a real traitor to me of late.

Artimus took a seat in one of the overstuffed brown leather chairs and pointed to another one. "Have a seat."

"I don't—" I began to protest.

His eyes went narrow once more. "Have a seat," came his stern interruption.

I wasn't afraid of Artimus. Hell, we were both around the same size and build. I could hold my own if he and I got physical. But I didn't want that to happen, so I took a seat and another sip. I felt a little bit calmer as I said, "I know you mean well, but I can't do this anymore. I'm losing too much."

"And how is that?" he asked, taking a sip of the Scotch before putting the short crystal glass down on the side table next to him.

I didn't want to tell him about anything. I knew it would sound insane. But I also knew he wasn't going to just let me do what I felt I had to without hearing some kind of an explanation for it. "I know that you think the best thing for me is to go see a shrink. But I know what that Patel woman will want to do to me."

He looked at me with concern etching his expression. "You do?"

"Yes, I do." I took another drink then put the glass down. "I haven't told you everything about my fiancée. Her name was Natalia Reddy."

"Yes, I'd heard that from Julia and Lila—they do talk a lot, you know" He shook his head as he looked down at the floor. "The fact that you never told me her name has never sat well with me. It made me think that I haven't been a very good friend to you. I should've asked more about her. I know that now."

"I've kept her all to myself for years now. Only recently have I shared more about her." I pushed my hand through my hair as I recalled the conversations I'd had with Nina about my fiancée. "And I did that with Nina. I don't know how she got it out of me, but she did. And now it feels like, because of that, she's pushed Natalia into the far recesses of my brain. I don't want her pushed back there. I want her up front, where she's always been since the moment I met her."

Artimus still didn't get it. "If your fiancée was alive, I could see that," he said. "But since she isn't, then it makes no sense. Nina didn't push anyone out of your head. Nina didn't force you to tell her things about Natalia, you just did. You did that because you felt like you could trust Nina. And you *can* trust her."

"I can't trust her." My hands fisted at my sides as I thought about how things had gone. "I forgot all about Natalia on the most important day. The day of her death." Raising my head, I glared at Artimus. "Why should I get to enjoy a carefree life while the woman I loved more than life itself is dead? Especially when I'm the reason she's not here anymore."

"The car accident wasn't your fault," he said as he shook his head. "And if you will just talk to that therapist, you will be able to see that you are allowed to live again. She can help you. Just try it and see."

"I don't want to try it." With a deep sigh, I let him in on things I hadn't before. "You see, I know what any therapist will do. They'll try to get me to forget Natalia. They'll tell me to live my life and leave her behind. Well, I don't want to leave her behind. I want to keep her right where she is. Or was, before Nina came into my life."

"Nina's been in your life for quite some time now. She's not to blame for anything. You know that. So stop blaming her. That girl doesn't deserve this. She's been nothing but good to you, and the way you're treating her is unacceptable." He leaned forward, looking at me with what I could only call wisdom in his eyes. "It's time to do what's right. Nina doesn't expect you to be with her. She's never expected anything out of you. She cares about you more than anyone else does. And for that, she's gotten the shit end of the deal here. If you aren't going to get better, then you need to tell her that. You need to let her go."

Guilt began to fill me. I had done Nina wrong. I knew I had. "I'm going to quit, Artimus. I can't work around her anymore. I can't do my job the way it needs to be done."

"I'm not about to accept your resignation, Ashton." He picked up his glass and took a drink, looking like he was pondering what his next move would be.

I wasn't waiting for him to get the jump on me. "You can't stop me from quitting, Artimus. Don't fool yourself into thinking that you can.

Being around Nina makes me think I can be normal. Be in a normal relationship again. I can't do that. Not when—"

He stopped me as he said, "Not when Natalia is dead. Yeah, yeah, I get it. But what you don't get is that I'm not going to sit here and let you do this to yourself." He got up and began to pace in front of me. "How could I call myself your friend if I let you quit your job and go off to do God knows what, and eventually lose everything you have? How could I call myself your friend if I allowed you to fall off into some abyss just so that you can what? Die yourself? Be a homeless bum?"

"I was managing to cope with things just fine before I went and thought I could have something more with Nina. I can go back to that. If I'm not around her, that is." I got up and went to look out the window at the busy street full of people. "For nearly four years, I've managed to get by. I can do it again, once Nina is out of my life."

"So Natalia can come back in?" Artimus came and put his hand on my shoulder. "You told me once that you would wake up screaming from nightmares at least once a week. And those nightmares were about the wreck and Natalia's death. On top of you momentarily forgetting about the date of the accident, are you saying that those dreams have stopped now?"

"They have." I closed my eyes and wished I could have those dreams again.

"And you think that Nina is the reason they've stopped?" he asked.

"She is." I opened my eyes then turned to look at my friend. "Nina is the one who fills my dreams now. I can't stop having dreams about her and me ..." I didn't know if I should tell him what I had dreamt about.

It didn't matter in the end, because he told me what he thought I was dreaming about. "Her and you having sex, I bet."

All I could do was nod. My throat felt as if it was closing up. I turned away from him to look out the window once more. It helped to watch the people down on the ground. It took my mind away from all the pain I felt.

"And you're saying you'd rather have nightmares about the worst day of your life, than have sex dreams about Nina?" he scoffed. I could hear the disbelief in his voice, and when he put it like that, it did sound crazy.

But he just didn't understand what it was like.

I heard Artimus as he walked away from me. I thought that meant he'd given up and was going to ease up on me. But when I heard him making a phone call, I realized I'd been mistaken. "Dr. Patel, this is Artimus Wolfe. We talked earlier about my friend and employee, Ashton Lange."

I couldn't breathe as I turned to look at him. "What are you doing?"

He didn't look at me at all as he went on. "Can I send my driver to pick you up and bring you here to my office? My friend is in need of your help. I would call this an emergency. He's ready to upend his entire life over the ghost of his fiancée."

Moving fast, I walked toward the door. He couldn't make me do anything I didn't want to.

Just as I got there, I heard a loud click. When I put my hand on the doorknob, it wouldn't move. "Artimus! What the hell are you doing?"

"See you soon, Dr. Patel." He ended the call then looked at me. "Saving you, Ashton. Someone has to do it. It might as well be me."

What the fuck?

CHAPTER FIFTEEN

Nina

I got home, took a long hot bath, and then climbed into my bed. It was all of seven o'clock, and I was done for the night. Not exactly what I had envisioned when I left work early.

My head wasn't into anything. All I wanted to do was stop thinking about Ashton Lange and how he'd made me feel. But I couldn't seem to do it.

A loud commotion in the living room had me climbing back out of bed to see what was going on. When I opened my bedroom door, I found my roommate, plus some company. Sandy had come in with two guys flanking her. "Oh, my bad. Are you sick, Nina?"

I looked down at my nightclothes. "Um, no. Just kind of worn out."

"You're home a lot earlier than usual. You should get dressed and come out with us," she urged me.

"Yeah, you should," the guy on her left said. "I feel like a third wheel."

"I don't know." I was never much one for going out. "Where are you guys going, anyway?"

Sandy came to me, taking me by the shoulders as she pushed me back into my bedroom. "Somewhere we can get our groove on. Now put on something tight and short that shows lots of skin."

The guy who must've thought he and I could be third wheels together chimed in, "I like red. And the name's Ty, by the way. Nice to meet you, Nina."

I didn't have a chance to respond, as Sandy had already pushed me into my room and forced me to sit on the bed. "I had better pick something out for you. You're good at picking out work clothes, but party clothes are not your forte."

"Sandy, I'm not really sure I'm up for partying. Not by your standards, anyway. I could probably just go for some wine and a little jazz."

I didn't go on with my idea of a good time, as Sandy shot me a look that told me I wasn't cool in the least. "Jazz? Wine? What are you, sixty?" With a toss of her head that sent blonde curls falling over her shoulder, she reached into my closet and pulled out a garment from a few years back. The sexy devil costume that I'd worn once for a Halloween party—and I hadn't even kept it on the whole time, having felt too uncomfortable.

"No." I shook my head furiously. "I should've thrown that away. That thing is tight and just too naughty."

She held it up to her chest. The red lace corset plunged into a V shape in the front. It left very little to the imagination. And when she found my black leather skirt to pair it with, I just couldn't stop shaking my head.

But she nodded. "Yes, this will look amazing on you. And I've got red heels that will match. All you need to do is gather your hair up in a messy ponytail and throw on some makeup, and we'll be good to go. As soon as I change, that is."

Peering out my bedroom door, I jerked my head toward it. "Hey, the Ty guy doesn't think this is a date, does he?"

"So what if he does?" Her hand went to her ample hip. "All that means is that you won't be paying for any of your drinks. There are worse things to have than an easy date for the night, girl."

"Yeah, but ..." I looked again, to be sure neither of those guys was listening to us. When I found no one anywhere near the door I went on, "Most guys think a date ends with a kiss, at the very least."

She laughed so loudly and abruptly that I jumped up and went to put my hand over her loud mouth. She pushed my hand back as her blue eyes danced. "Nina, stop being such a prude. One little kiss won't kill you. And if you're lucky ... well, then you'll get lucky."

But I didn't want to get lucky with anyone other than Ashton. And now, not even him. "I should just stay home. I'm going to ruin that guy's fun."

"No, you won't." She walked over to my door, kicked it shut then came at me. "If I have to put these clothes on you myself, then I will."

I laughed as she pushed me onto my bed and ripped my shorts right off. "I'll do it myself! God!"

Tossing the thin jersey shorts off to one side, she wagged her finger at me. "Hurry up. I want to get going. The night is young, and so are we."

She finally left me and I set to work, making myself slutty enough to meet Sandy's standards. It wasn't a look I usually went for, but I needed to make some changes anyway. I wasn't really going to be slutty. But I could look that way for a little while. And I could shake my ass for a few hours, if it helped me get my mind off things.

A mere half hour later I emerged from my room and found Ty and the guy who was supposed to be Sandy's date with their jaws gaping. I laughed at their expressions. "Come on, guys. Don't mess around with me."

Ty was quick to walk over to me. His hands took mine as he held me back and looked me over. "All I can say is I'm damn glad I came up here with those two and met you first. You're something else, baby."

"No." I pulled my hands out of his. "No baby. I'm Nina. You're Ty, and there will be no exchanging of sweet nicknames or anything like that."

"Sandy said you were single." He eyed me with his large dark eyes. He was cute, really. Tall, dark, and handsome enough. He smelled nice, and his beard was pretty cool too. But he didn't do it for me.

I suppose I had a type. Tall, muscular, blond, with eyes as blue as the Caribbean Sea. Ashton Lange was my type. Ty was nearly the polar opposite of the man that I was trying so hard to get out of my mind.

So, what better way to do that than to hang out with his polar opposite?

A little while later, we were walking into a dark nightclub where the music was blasting and people were dancing. And drinking. I saw a hell of a lot of drinking.

Ty bought a couple of drinks at the bar and handed me one. He took a drink and put mine to my mouth, urging me to drink up. Which I did. I needed something to take the edge off.

My heart wasn't in this at all. My mind knew I had to get out of my comfort zone, but my heart was telling me that I needed to take it easy. It was hurting; I needed some time.

But I'd given my heart too much time already.

Ty had my hand in his, and our drinks were in our other hands as he led me to the dancefloor. Gyrating to a hard beat wasn't the easiest thing for me to get into, but as I sipped on the fruity drink, it became easier and easier to do.

Sandy and her guy, who I found out was named Sloan, came up to dance near us. She kept flashing me smiles and nods, along with several thumbs-ups.

Watching Sandy dance was like watching porn. But that was how most of the people in the club were dancing too. It looked like they were dry humping each other. I imagined most of them actually were doing just that.

I had never been that kind of a dancer, preferring not to get that damn close to virtual strangers. Ty was being cool about it. He only pulled me close once. When I put my hand on his chest, he smiled and let me go. I supposed it was enough for him to be dancing with me, knowing that I wasn't going off with anyone else.

I wasn't, either. Before we'd gotten to the club I'd asked him to please not leave me to the wolves that night. So far, Ty was being a nice guy about it all.

But alcohol and dancing might take their toll on the guy, and who knew what would happen then?

It began to get hot, and I was relieved when Ty took my hand and led me out of the crowd. He took me to a quieter place in the club, and we sat at a table where a waitress came to ask us what we wanted to drink.

"A couple of gin and tonics," he ordered us.

I hadn't ever had one of those, but I was so thirsty I didn't care what type of wet liquid came to me. "Thanks, Ty. You're a pretty nice guy."

"Ya think?" His lips pulled up to one side as he sat back and draped his arm over the back of my chair.

"I hope," I corrected myself. "The truth is, I am single, but I've been crushing on this one guy for about two years now."

His dark brows shot up. "Two years?"

"Yeah." I turned my head as I felt my cheeks heat up with embarrassment at how surprised he was. "And recently, he made a move on me."

"So, where is he then?" he asked as he reached out to take my chin, pulling my face back to look at him.

"No, we're not a thing. He's afraid. But he has his reasons. I wasn't mad at him about it at all." I thought about how I was mad now though. "But he's been hiding from me, and that has made me mad." I frowned, both at the memory of Ashton storming away from me, and at how easily I was spilling my guts to this stranger.

"Hiding?" he asked, with confusion riddling his face. "From you? Why?" His eyes narrowed as he looked at me. "Are you crazy or something? Because that would be the only thing that would make any sense. You're a knockout. You've got to know that. You do have a mirror, right?"

I rolled my eyes at him. "I know I'm attractive, if that's what you're getting at." I found it odd that guys always thought that women just needed to know they were pretty and that would solve all their problems. I happened to believe that a woman should have a personality that was on the attractive side too. Having a nice personality was even more attractive than natural beauty, in my opinion.

The drinks came, and we downed them in record time. Ty had held up two fingers at the waitress when she dropped those off, so we had a couple more coming that we could sip on.

He put his empty glass on the table before I did. "Seems we were parched."

Putting my empty glass down, I agreed. "Seems so."

"So, this moron, what's his deal?" he asked me as he sat back and once again draped his arm over the back of my chair.

"He's not a moron," I corrected him. "He's just had a really rough few years. That said, tragic past or not, that doesn't excuse his behavior of late."

With a shrug, Ty said, as if it were the easiest thing in the world, "My advice is to forget about this guy. Two years is too long, if you ask me. He had his chance, and he messed it up. Time to move on." He curled a chunk of my hair around his index finger. "And I'm right here. I think you're gorgeous and nice, to boot. One hell of a combination, and a rare one at that. In New York, anyway."

When his dark eyes caught mine and his went soft and sultry, I had a feeling I knew what was coming. When his head began to move closer to mine, I knew I was right.

And I knew I wasn't going to let it happen. Not because he wasn't nice. Not because he wasn't cute.

It was because he wasn't Ashton.

CHAPTER SIXTEEN

Ashton

To say I was pissed at Artimus for bringing in a shrink as he held me captive in his office would be an understatement. But as mad as I was, I didn't take it out on him. He was doing what he thought a friend should do.

But I also wasn't promising to give this Jasmine Patel woman more than one session with me. As soon as the words came out of her mouth, telling me that I had to put Natalia behind me, I was going to let her know that I did not need her services.

"I will leave you to it then, Dr. Patel," Artimus said as soon as she arrived.

Sitting in one of the chairs, I almost didn't bother to get up. But then I knew that would be rude of me, and I went to her with my hand extended. "Ashton Lange, Dr. Patel. It's nice to meet you."

"It's so nice to meet you too, Mr. Lange." She gestured to the chairs. "Please, sit, and let's get comfortable while you tell me all about this fiancée of yours."

Taking a seat, I began, "Natalia Reddy stole my heart from the moment I laid eyes on her. And getting to know her only cemented in my heart the love I had for her. And that is where I plan to keep her."

She had a pad of paper and a pen in hand, but she didn't write down anything that I'd just said. Instead, she smiled at me. "Of course you want to keep her in your heart. She belongs there. Her body is no more, but she is still with you in many ways. She always will be, Mr. Lange." Adjusting herself in the chair to get more comfortable, she crossed her legs at the ankles and took a more laid-back stance. "I am not here to erase your fiancée. I don't want you to worry about that, or get defensive with me. I am only here to help you."

That did make me feel more comfortable with her, though I was still a little on edge. She'd been a bit too on the nose with that, and it made me wonder if Artimus had somehow had a chance to talk to her beforehand and tell her my fears. "Thank you. I was deeply afraid that anyone in your profession would think I needed to get Natalia out of my head and heart in order to move on with my life."

"You must learn to absorb her better." A wide smile moved across her face. She wasn't old, but she wasn't young either. Maybe in her late thirties. Maybe she could help me after all. "I need to let you know a bit about what you may be dealing with here. A number of research studies have proven that spousal bereavement is a major source of life stress that often leaves people vulnerable to later problems, including depression, chronic stress, and even reduced life expectancy."

That was news to me. "I could have a shortened life expectancy?"

"You could if you don't get help, Mr. Lange." With a brief nod, she went on. "The grief process commonly takes months, sometimes years, to subside. There are a small number of people who experience symptoms for a much longer period of time. In some cases, these symptoms resemble other psychiatric conditions such as Major Depressive Disorder, also called MDD. At times it can be impossible to tell if a person is suffering from the disorder or just suffering from grief."

It was hard to believe that I had a disorder. "I have Major Depressive Disorder? I've always considered myself a happy guy."

"I didn't say you have MDD," she clarified herself. "I said the symptoms of that disorder are the same as the grieving process. Now tell me, and answer honestly, please, did you cry after her death?"

"I cried a lot. And I do mean a lot." In the beginning, it was almost nonstop. "And at times I still do."

Now her pen went to the pad of paper on her lap. "Can you tell me when the last time you cried over her was?"

"A little over two weeks ago." I recalled the last time I'd dreamt about her. "I woke up from a dream about her that ended with the crash that took her away from me. I've had that dream about once a week for the past four years, and every time I wake up screaming and crying for her to wake up. But I'm okay with that."

Shaking her head, she wrote something down about that. "You shouldn't be okay with that."

"I'm not here to lose Natalia, Dr. Patel." It was time to be truthful with the woman. "I'm here to get this other woman off my mind so my fiancée can come back into it."

"No," came her quick response as she kept writing things down about me.

No? "What do you mean, no?"

She looked up from the paper to look me in the eyes with a stern expression. "I will not help you to live an unhealthy life, Mr. Lange. I am here to help you. Now, please tell me how often you've expressed your grief to anyone else?"

I had talked to Nina and Duke, and even Artimus about Natalia. But I had never cried with them or anything like that. Nor anyone else for that matter. I kept it all to myself. "Um, I don't share it."

I had earned another shake of her head. "Ah, but you need to share it."

"I've shared more about Natalia with the woman I'm currently trying to get off my mind than I have with anyone else," I confided in her. "But I definitely don't want to talk to her about it anymore. It made me feel close to her. It made me start fantasizing about her. It made me dream about her instead of Natalia."

After jotting down more notes, she looked at me with concern, her voice echoing that same emotion, "What do you think is wrong with feeling close to someone?"

I thought about that for a long moment before answering, "It wouldn't be so bad, but it's pushing Natalia out. I don't want her pushed out."

"She's no longer here, Mr. Lange," she felt the need to point out.

"She was," I said. "At least in my dreams. That is until I went and shared her memory with Nina. Now she's gone."

More scribbling on the paper. So much that she had to turn to a new page to keep on writing. I knew it was pretty bad if she was doing all that writing. "Where are Natalia's things, Mr. Lange?"

"All I have of her now is a picture of her that I keep in my wallet." I pulled my wallet out to get the picture and show it to her. Leaning forward, I let her see it, and she nodded before I put it away. "Her family came and took all of her things away. They said it would help me heal faster."

"Ah!" She pointed a finger in the air as if she'd found the solution. Which I'd hoped she had. "I do believe we've stumbled upon something here, Mr. Lange. You see, it's important for the spouse who's left behind to be able to hold onto the personal possessions that the deceased left behind. It should've been left up to you to decide when and what you would get rid of that belonged to Natalia. I am sure they didn't mean to harm you in any way, but they did harm you. That is a critical step in the grieving process."

"I did feel way more out of it after they came and took everything away," I recalled. "It had only been five days since her death when they did that. It was her father who thought it would help me. I couldn't get out of bed after the accident. I did manage to pull my ass out of bed long enough to attend her funeral, which was only 36 hours after she'd passed away. I felt it was all happening way too fast. The only other funeral I had ever attended was that of my grandfather, and it was held three days after his death. They did everything so damn fast. I felt lost."

Her eyes became soft and caring. "I believe your fiancée was Hindu? That is the Hindu way, Mr. Lange. Were you unaware of that aspect of her and her family's religious beliefs?"

"Very unaware, I guess. It all hit me so hard. Everything just moved so fast, and everyone seemed in such a hurry to get things done. It never made sense to me," I finally admitted it. I had never even thought about how I felt back then. "It was like I was watching a movie or something. Things happened that I wasn't a part of. It was all so disconcerting."

"While we cannot go back in time to change everything that happened, we can do it mentally," she let me know. "We have our starting point, Mr. Lange. Your healing can now begin. Natalia doesn't belong in your dreams all the time, or even once a week the way you think she does. She has a place in your memory though, and in your heart, always. And it's my opinion, as your therapist, that you should nurture any friendship with someone who you feel you're able to share this part of your past with—even the woman you spoke of earlier."

She had no idea how afraid I was of Nina, and of what might happen between us. "But what if I fall in love with her in the process?"

"Then good for you both." She threw her hands up in the air. "Love is wonderful. And if you do get the chance to fall in love not once, but twice, you are doubly blessed."

"If that's so, then why do I feel so afraid when I think of love?" I had to ask her that, because I couldn't quite figure it out myself.

"Because you have healing left to do over the loss you've suffered." With a nod, she came to a conclusion, "In my opinion, you do not suffer from MDD at all. But you are suffering from grief. Healing and grief, they're both processes, and there's no telling when they start and when they end. But you're doing a very good thing by sitting here and talking with me, and we'll be able to help you move forward with your life."

She had already helped me more than I'd expected. But I hadn't been completely honest with her. "Dr. Patel, there's more. Before you go and count out the MDD thing."

Her brows lifted. "More?"

"Yes, more." I swallowed hard because I knew this was big. "You see, I was driving that day. It had begun to rain, and the car slipped on the road. I lost control and ended up in the median, hitting a tree. That's when Natalia was killed. It was my fault."

Her eyes went to the floor. She made a long, deep sigh before saying. "That is indeed a tragic accident." Then she looked right into my eyes. "Do you understand the meaning of the word accident, Mr. Lange?"

"I do. But I also know there were a number of things I could've done to prevent that accident from occurring." And here I was again, trying to explain to someone who had no clue what it felt like to have the blood of someone you love on your hands.

It just didn't wash away that damn easily.

When she stood up, I thought she was going to leave. Instead, she pulled up the sleeve of her shirt, and I saw a long, jagged scar on the inside of her arm. "This is from an injury I sustained when I was nineteen. It was the middle of the night. Everyone was asleep in my home. My parents, my grandparents, my six sisters, and my brothers too. I woke to the smell of smoke." Her eyes were glued to mine. "The curtain in my bedroom was on fire. Flames shot up the wall, and in no time, they traveled to the ceiling. I didn't tell anyone what was happening."

"Why not?" I asked.

"Because I had been smoking marijuana in my bedroom earlier that night. When I fell asleep, the joint fell out of my fingers, down to the floor beside my bed, and lit the curtain on fire." Her lips formed one straight line as she let that sink in before she went on, "That fire engulfed our entire home. Thankfully, my father had installed smoke alarms in the home, and they all got out before anyone was hurt."

I pointed at her arm. "That doesn't explain the scar."

Shaking her head, she said, "No, it doesn't. Because this is the rest of that story. I couldn't get out of my bedroom. The fire trapped me in. And there's more. I had my six-month-old baby in the room with me. I finally managed to break the glass in one of my windows, and I cut my arm when I pulled it back in after passing my baby through the window to my mother, who had come to find us."

"Oh. So, you felt guilt about burning down the family home." It wasn't quite the same as my guilt, but I understood where she was coming from.

"Yes, I felt guilt over that. But what nearly killed me was the death of my baby girl, Mr. Lange. She died of smoke inhalation that night. And that was entirely my fault." She took her seat again, still holding her head high and looking at me. "That was my firstborn child. I loved her more than life itself. I cried for weeks, then months, then an entire year went by, and finally, the tears began to subside. But my love for her has never stopped. It never will. I now have a husband and four children. Do you think I am wrong for moving on, Mr. Lange?"

Hell, no!

CHAPTER SEVENTEEN

Nina

Saturday morning, I woke up with a hangover and decided to go right back to sleep. I slept that day away, and then later that night, Sandy tried in vain to get me to go out again. I wasn't about to do a repeat of Friday night. "No way."

"Come on, Nina. You had fun last night. Admit it, already." She tossed a glossy black pump onto my bed, which I was still lying in. "You can borrow these, if you want to."

"Why would I do that? My feet still hurt from the pair of heels I borrowed from you last night." I sat up to pull one of my feet up so that I could massage it. "Besides, Ty and I left on good terms at the end of the night. If I go out again and he's there—"

"He will be. He's coming with Sloan and me again," she interrupted me. "And he said he really hoped you would come along too. He likes you, you know."

"He's a good guy." I had to give him that. He hadn't put any pressure on me at all. But I didn't want to hang out with anyone or go out. I just didn't feel up to it. "But I'm out for tonight. We'll see what next weekend brings."

Sandy gave me puppy dog eyes. "He's going to be disappointed."

"Well, he better get used to it where I'm concerned. He may as well get that out of the way now." I knew Ty would take all the slack I gave him. I didn't want to lead the man on, though.

Eventually Sandy left me alone, and I started reading a book. It was a real page-turner about an ex-Marine who had found a lost love. One who had secretly had his baby a few years back. The poor guy had PTSD and it made for a really hard time in making his newly found family work.

I stayed up till three in the morning to finish the book, but it was worth it. When I put my Kindle away, I thought about the story I had read. Ashton kind of had the same kind of problem as the main character. He'd had a tragedy in his life that had altered him.

The anger he'd shown hadn't made any sense to me before, but I thought I was coming to understand it a bit more.

He and I had gotten along great that weekend. It must have done something to trigger him in some way. I was sure something had to have sprung forward in his mind that had him wanting to stay away from me.

What I couldn't understand was why he didn't think he could talk to me about it. He and I had been friends too long for him to just turn away from me. First and foremost, I was his friend. He knew that.

When sleep finally found me, I dreamt about a car wreck. It wasn't apparent who was involved. It was as if I was watching from above. Like in a helicopter or something.

People were rushing everywhere as a car burned. Sirens wailed, police cars and ambulances showed up. In the end, one lone figure slumped against a police car. The pain and anguish reached me through the dream, and I woke up crying.

The sun was shining through the window, letting me know it had only been a dream. But that pain and misery were still working on me. It felt terrible.

A hot shower helped me get rid of the lingering memory of the dream. I made some breakfast. Bagels and cream cheese with a glass of apple juice to start my day.

Grabbing my laundry, I got busy taking care of the mundane, typical Sunday chores. Cleaning my bedroom, washing the laundry, then sprucing up the living room and kitchen made the day go by fast.

With nothing else to do after dinner, I looked for a new book to read on my Kindle. A knock at the door stole my attention away from the device, however. "Now who could that be?"

It was about seven in the evening. I hadn't expected anyone to be coming over. Both of my roommates were out too, so no one would be coming to see them.

Putting down the Kindle, I went to answer the door. Looking out the peephole, I saw a face that made me smile before I could stop myself and remember all the reasons why I shouldn't be smiling at him.

I opened the door, and a huge bouquet of red roses filled my sight. "It's me. The jackass. I've come to beg for your forgiveness." The flowers lowered, and there was Ashton's handsome face. "Can you ever forgive me, Nina?"

I stepped back to allow him to come in. "Maybe. Care to plead your case?"

He came in and placed a kiss on my cheek as he passed me. "I will explain it all to you." Putting the vase of flowers on the coffee table, he pulled a box of chocolates out of his jacket and placed them next to it. "I thought candy might help too."

"It never hurts." I took a seat and grabbed the box to see what kind of candy it had in it. "Yes, I love the kind with lots of nuts. You did good, Ashton."

He took a seat on the chair across from me. "Glad to hear that. After a week of doing terribly, hearing that I'm doing well is a relief."

As I unwrapped a peanut cluster, I eyed him. He looked a little different to me. "So, what happened to you?" I was pretty glad I'd read that book the night before. It had turned a lot of my anger into empathy, though I was still ready to hear him grovel a little for my forgiveness.

His blue eyes cut away from me. I knew he was kind of embarrassed by the way he'd acted. "Nina, I wanted to be away from you because I was blaming you for something."

"Did I do something I wasn't aware of?" I asked him, then popped the chocolate into my mouth.

He nodded, making me raise my eyebrow. I couldn't think of what the heck I might've done. "You see, I really like you."

"Okay. That's not a bad thing." I picked up my bottle of water off the table. "You want something to drink? I've got water, and I think I've got beer in there too."

"No," he said as he shook his head. "I'm okay. I just want to get this off my chest."

"Sure. Go ahead." I waited to hear what he had to say.

The way he hesitated told me he was finding it hard to start, but he finally did. "I had a lot of fun last weekend with you. And all that fun made me forget a day that's been the most important day in my life for a few years now. I was reminded finally of what day it was when the guys and I went to the pub while you girls were shopping. Sunday was the anniversary of Natalia's death."

Now I understood completely. My hand flew to my cover my mouth, empathizing with the pain and confusion he must've felt. "Oh, God."

He got up and came to sit next to me. His hand on my shoulder sent chills through me. "Nina, I got mad at you because being with you made me forget everything else. It was wrong of me to act that way toward you, and it was wrong of me to put that blame on you. You see, I used to dream about her. Now I only dream about you."

My heart leapt with the news. But it also ached because I knew he wasn't wholly pleased by it—I knew the dreams were part of his grief and remembrance for his fiancée. "Ashton, I'm sorry you're hurt by that."

His eyes crept up to meet mine, and I saw so much more in them than I had before. "I'm sure you are. I'm getting help now. I'm seeing a therapist. I'm not ready for romance, but I really need my friend back. Do you think you can be my friend again, Nina?"

I was about to cry. The tears were welling up in my eyes. All I could do was reach out and hug him. "I can be your friend, Ashton. I can always be that for you."

We hugged for a minute, holding each other tight. The attraction was still there, but I wanted him to feel my concern for him more than I wanted him to feel my hunger.

"Thank you, Nina. I really am sorry for how I treated you this last week." He pulled back and took my chin in his hand. "I was just afraid, is all."

"Afraid of me taking Natalia's place." I nodded. "I want you to know that I'll never be the kind of person who'd want to replace her like that. I'm not jealous of her. And I never will be." I hoped that what I was saying would always be true. I never wanted to make him feel bad about having love for another woman. Not when she wasn't around anymore to even be worried about.

The most important thing was that we had our friendship back.

CHAPTER EIGHTEEN

Ashton

No longer dreading Monday after having spoken to Nina, I was in a pretty great mood when I walked into the station that morning. I felt renewed. Not one hundred percent over my grief and guilt, but ready to start working through it.

I had an apology ready for Artimus, so I went right up to his office. When the elevator doors opened, Brady and Veronica stood perfectly still, looking at me.

Hesitantly, Brady offered, "Good morning?" in question form.

After Friday's tirade, I understood his cautious demeanor. "It is a good morning, Brady. How's it going this morning for you guys?"

Veronica nodded. "Fine. Are you here to see someone, Ashton?"

"I am. Has Artimus made it in yet?" I made my way toward his door, sure he was already in. He always showed up early.

"He is," Brady told me. "Julia is in there with him."

"Good." I knocked on the door, ready to make amends with my friend.

"Come in," came Julia's voice as the door opened.

Artimus got up out of his seat to come to me. "I hope you're not mad."

Shaking my head as I went to shake his hand, I said, "Anything but that." We shook hands then I went in for a little side hug. "Thank you, Artimus. It takes a great friend to do what you did. Dr. Patel is the best. I've talked to her extensively every day since Friday. I know things are going to get better, with her help."

Julia grabbed me up as I stepped away from Artimus. "That's so great to hear, Ashton!" She hugged me tightly, swaying back and forth with me. "I'm so happy for you."

"I'm pretty damn happy for myself too." When she let me go, I saw Artimus waving at me to go sit down in front of his desk, so I went over and took a seat as he sat behind it. "Just so you guys know, I went to see Nina and apologized to her too. We're not dating, but we are friends again."

"Good." Julia walked toward the door that connected their offices. "I've got to get to work. You guys talk. See you later, Ashton. We'll have to do lunch together today."

"Sure thing, Julia." I waved at her then looked at Artimus. "With Dr. Patel's help, I've made a big discovery about why I've held on the way I have."

"And that is?" he asked.

"Natalia's things were taken from our home way too soon after her passing. Her family thought it would help me." I sighed as I thought about what good people they all were. "They didn't mean any harm in doing it, but it interrupted my grieving process. This weekend I made a call to her father and asked about some of those things. He told me that most of her stuff had been given to people in need. And that made me happy. Natalia would've wanted her things to go to good use, not sit around like museum pieces."

I had earned a smile from Artimus. "Good. I'm really glad to hear that you're happy with how that went. I suppose them removing all of her things from your place really set you back. I mean, one day she's there with you, the next she's gone. And not long after that, all evidence of her ever being there was gone too. I can see how that would shake a person up."

Shoving my hand through my hair, I tried to do what Dr. Patel had asked me to work on. Live in that moment. Let myself feel that pain. And share it with those I care about and who care about me. "I had pushed the memories of that time into the far recesses of my mind. Next to actually losing her, losing her things in our home was the second most traumatic thing I went through. And the weird thing is that I never told a single soul how bad that hurt, to look around and see nothing of hers in our home anymore. Even the shampoo and conditioner she used was gone."

Artimus looked stricken as he looked down. "I can't imagine, Ashton. That had to have been devastating to you. I don't know if I could've taken that."

"You could've. I mean, it doesn't kill you." I shook my head. "But it feels like it might."

With a nod, he said, "I'm sure it did feel like that. And how are you handling that now?"

I had to smile. "Better. Nina and I talked until one o'clock this morning. I shared a lot with her about Natalia. It made me feel a hell of a lot better. Nina is a very special person."

"She is." He laughed. "Most women wouldn't have hung on for so long. You know that, right?"

"I do." I had more I wanted to talk to him about, but wasn't sure how. Then I took the good doctor's advice and just opened my mouth and said what was on my mind. "I'm still afraid, Artimus. I'm still afraid that letting myself fall for Nina will push Natalia out of my mind."

"I don't think she'll allow that to happen, Ashton." He shook his head. "Nina isn't the type of person who tries to take over things. I believe she has, and always has had, your best interests at heart."

"You're probably right." I got up; it was time to get to work. "Well, I've got to get busy this morning. I am sorry for my little meltdown last week."

"Nothing to worry about. We all have our meltdowns now and

then, Ashton. And if that's what it took for you to finally accept help, then I'm glad." He got up and walked with me to the door, clapping me on the back as we went. "You have a good day. I'll see you at lunch."

I left there feeling a lot better about things. And a hell of a lot better about my ability to let my friends in on what was bothering me. I had kept it all to myself for way too long. It felt good to confide in my friend for once.

When I went down to the set where the morning news was about to get underway, I found Nina finishing up the cue cards on the long table she always kept them on.

One of the cameramen stopped me before I could get to her. "Hey, Ashton. Man, glad you came down this morning. I need you to take a look at this camera. It seems to be malfunctioning a little."

I took a look and fixed the problem, then found it was time to get the show started. Taking my usual chair at the back of the studio, I counted down the time for the show to start.

Nina bent over the table to stay out of the camera's view. I had to admire her round bottom, which was covered in a creamy fabric that clung to it just right.

As everyone got going, I zoned out, seeing Nina bent over just as she was, only in my office, bent over my desk. She looked over her shoulder at me as she hitched the beige skirt up and bit her lower lip.

I moved in behind her, cupping her bare ass cheeks in both hands as I took a long sniff along her neck. The scent of honeysuckle filled my nostrils as I ran my lips along the side of her neck. Her ass blossomed with goosebumps as I rubbed it.

"Commercial, Ashton," my assistant whispered in my ear.

Shit!

I gave the sign to cut to the commercial and everyone loosened up for the two-minute break. Nina stood up and turned to look at me. She gave me a little wave, and I waved back.

As soon as the news program was over, I went to Nina. "Come to my office when you can, okay?"

With a nod, she picked up her cards and took them with her. "I'll be there in about fifteen minutes. I've just got to shred these first and get them into the recycle bin."

I had brought a gift for her. The night before, I'd given her roses and candy. But I wanted to give her the present I'd bought for her before I lost my mind that Sunday.

When she came into my office, I was surprised to see that she had a gift-wrapped box in her hands. Pointing at it, I asked, "For me?"

She nodded as she placed it on my desk. I opened the drawer where I'd put the gift for her. It was in a little pink bag, and I put it on the desk in front of her.

She smiled. "Seems like great minds do think alike."

I took my present and she took hers then we both opened them. "Oh, wow!" She'd given me the same kind of pan that we'd found at Artimus and Julia's home to make bacon in.

"I saw that and thought of you." She winked at me. "Maybe you can make me some bacon sometime."

Jerking my head toward the bag she had her hand in, I said, "Maybe I will. Come on, pull that out of there. I'm dying to see what you think of it."

When she pulled out the expensive wrap she'd eyed at the market in the Hamptons, a smile took over her whole face. "You didn't!"

"I did." I took it out of her hands, then wrapped it around her neck, tying it in front. "Look, it even matches this outfit."

Her lips touched my cheek, sending a charge of energy from my cheek all the way down to my cock, which thumped in response. "I love it. Thank you."

I kissed her cheek, straining my cock even more. "Thank you too."

Her hand went to rest on my chest as we stood close together. Her eyes moved up to mine as she bit her lower lip. It was the same look she'd given me in my little daydream earlier.

My eyes cut away from hers to look at my desk. It wasn't at all the way I'd seen it in my fantasy. It was cluttered with papers and all kinds of other things. Sweeping it all away would've had a dramatic effect, but a messy one.

And I didn't want to ravage Nina in my office anyway. She deserved better than that.

Taking her by the wrists, I looked at her, then sighed. I wasn't going to bring her into my cluttered world at the moment. I had a lot more work to do on myself before I did that. "We're all going to eat lunch together today. You should come too."

She licked her lips. "Okay. I will."

My body was on fire, and I knew she was the only thing in the world that could put it out. But I couldn't do that to her. Not until I had myself straightened out completely. I'd already put her through enough. "I would love a cup of that coffee of yours, if you make any today."

"I will, and I'll bring you a cup." Her breasts rose and fell as she took a deep breath. "I want you to know that above all else, I am your friend, Ashton. Last night, when you were so open with me, it made me feel so much closer to you than I've ever felt. Thank you for letting me in. It's an honor and a privilege to me."

Her dark blonde hair had fallen into her face a bit, and I brushed it back. "I want to thank you for being there for me. The honor is all mine to have you as a friend, Nina Kramer."

I meant every word I said to her. And a kiss at that moment would've felt perfectly right.

But I rarely did what was right.

Stepping back, I walked away from her to get behind my desk. "See you later, then."

A brief look of confusion filled her face, then she nodded. "Yes, I'll come back later with the coffee."

Watching her sweet ass sway back and forth as she left my office, I looked down at my erect cock. "What? She deserves me at my best. You'll just have to wait."

CHAPTER NINETEEN

Nina

The week went by and everything was going great. Better than great. But that Friday, things were about to get even better.

Ashton came to my office and walked right in. "Hey, you."

I looked up from my computer. "Hi there."

It was nearly noon, and I figured he was there to walk with me to the studio to do the afternoon newscast. So, I got up to leave with him.

But his hands on my shoulders stopped me. "Where do you think you're going, Nina?"

"Um, to the studio. Isn't that what you're here for?" I asked.

He shook his head. "No. You're off for the weekend, starting right now."

"And why is that?" I asked, as a thrill ran through me.

He looked over his shoulder then kicked the door closed. His eyes ran over me before settling back on my own. "I want to ask you something. And please be honest."

"Of course."

"I'm not one hundred percent over things. But Dr. Patel tells me that waiting to be perfect is a mistake. So I'm not going to wait anymore." His eyes closed, and my heart raced. When he opened them, he asked, "Can we start dating?"

"Yes!" flew out of my mouth without me even thinking about it for a second. And I was ready for the kiss I had been waiting for too.

"Good." He did kiss me, but only on the cheek. "I've set up a pretty great date for us tonight. But your part of it will start now. I've booked you a spa day. Artimus has been gracious enough to let us use his driver and town car. They'll take you to the spa, where you'll get the full treatment. There are a couple of packages in the trunk of that car for you too. Those are my gifts to you, and I would like for you to wear them to dinner."

"You're treating me like a princess, Ashton." I was in awe. But I didn't want him to think I was that kind of girl who had to be spoiled and pampered. "You don't have to do all this."

"I know I don't have to." He kissed my other cheek. "I want to. Let me do this."

Who was I to argue?

"Okay. So, what time should I be ready for dinner?" I asked, as my mind raced ahead of me.

"Eight. We have an eight-thirty reservation at The River Café in Brooklyn." His smile was huge, knowing that he had really pulled out all the stops.

"Wow. A spa day and a meal at a prestigious restaurant?" I was on cloud nine as he walked me to the waiting car outside the station.

A quick kiss to my forehead and I was on my way to one remarkable day.

After being soaked and scrubbed in various things and massaged into a blissful state, I came home and put on the little black dress he'd bought for me. Matching pumps came with it. And a smaller box held a set of diamond earrings and a necklace.

Standing in front of my full-length mirror, I barely recognized myself. And when I went out into the living room to wait for Ashton, I found Sandy, Sloan, and Ty having themselves a few beers before heading out for their night of fun.

Ty looked me up and down as he whistled. "Do you clean up nice or what, Nina?"

Sandy's mouth was hanging open. "Where did you get all that, Nina? And are those real diamonds?"

"They are," I said with a nod. "Ashton gave them to me. We're going on our first date—finally. He's taking me out to The River Café in Brooklyn for dinner tonight. And he sent me to the spa today too."

Ty sounded a little grumpy as he said, "So, this guy's got a shit-ton of money, then. I never stood a chance in hell."

Shaking my head, I corrected him, "No, you didn't stand a chance. But not because Ashton is rich. I mean, he's doing well for himself, but that's not why you never stood a chance against him. I've got it bad for him. I told you that. And now, he's finally showing me how bad he's got it for me too."

Ty smiled then and came to kiss my cheek. "He's one lucky SOB."

"Thanks, Ty." A knock at the door had me turning around. "I bet that's him."

Peeking out the peephole, I saw Ashton wearing a black suit and tie and looking like a million dollars. I opened the door, and he reached out to take my hand. "You look amazing, Nina. I knew you would." He fingered the necklace that he'd given me. "It all looks perfect on you, just the way I imagined it."

Sandy cleared her throat. "Hi there."

I turned to introduce Ashton to everyone. "This is my roommate, Sandy. And that's Sloan standing next to her. And this is Ty." Ty had come up to stand behind me.

He reached out to shake Ashton's hand. "Hi."

Ashton looked a little confused as he said, "Hi. Nice to meet you guys."

"So, you're taking her out to a fancy dinner, huh?" Ty asked.

Ashton nodded. "I am."

"What time are you going to have her back home?" Ty asked.

I laughed and pulled on Ashton's hand. "Come on, Ashton. He's just kidding around with you. Night, guys. Be careful out there." I closed the door behind us.

As we went to the elevator, Ashton looked at me with a puzzled expression. "And who is he to you, Nina?"

"I think he has the hots for me. But he's a nice guy. No one to worry about," I let him know.

"Okay. If you say so." Ashton pushed the button on the elevator and off we went to our first official night out.

The restaurant was even better than I expected. The ambience was amazing, and so was the food.

The waiter brought us a bottle of wine—a '07 Alfred Gratien Cuvee Paradis from France, which cost $230 a bottle. After our glasses were filled, I leaned in close to whisper to Ashton, "You really are breaking the bank for this date, aren't you?"

When his fingertips grazed along my jawline, I nearly melted in my chair. "I want to show you how much I appreciate and care for you." His lips barely touched my ear. "Baby."

The way the term of endearment made my stomach flip gave me all kinds of ideas about things to come.

This night is going to be a dream!

The appetizer arrived and my eyes went wide as saucers as I looked at the marvelous creation that was set before us. Named Three Shells, it consisted of a variety of chilled shellfish. Fresh abalone was garnished with citrus, soy, and lime. Kumamoto oysters were covered in cucumber champagne mignonette. Then Taylor Bay scallop ceviche was mixed with sea bean, tomato, and coriander.

Ashton fed me a tiny bite of each. He had no idea the effect he was having on me as he placed the food in my mouth. "It's fantastic."

I picked up a tiny fork and stabbed a scallop, then fed it to him. He moaned as he chewed it. "You're right, it is amazing."

The appetizer alone was enough, but there was more to come.

The main courses were just as decadent. He had black sea bass that had been sautéed with lobster brown butter. It was served with grilled artichoke ravioli and fresh artichoke.

I had poached Nova Scotia lobster. It came with sweet and sour butternut squash risotto, Trumpet Royale mushrooms, and even brussels sprout leaves.

"This meal is so impressive." I finished off the last bite, cleaning my plate.

He looked at the empty plate with a smile on his face. "I'm impressed too. And now for dessert."

The only thing I wanted for dessert was him.

But he'd already ordered, it seemed. Our waiter came and cleared our plates as the dessert was delivered by a very proud dessert chef. "Our famous Chocolate Brooklyn Bridge. It's made with milk chocolate Marquise, raspberry sorbet, vanilla ice cream, crisp meringue, and topped with a dark chocolate glaze."

"It's gorgeous," I remarked. "I'm sure it tastes as good as it looks too."

The chef nodded, then left us to enjoy the decadent treat.

Ashton spoon-fed me once more. I gave him bites too, and it was obvious by the glow on his cheeks that he was getting as turned on as I was.

Picking up his napkin, he ran it over my lips. "Some extra chocolate got away from you." Then his lips touched the spot right next to mine, and I nearly turned to capture his lips.

I didn't though. The longing I felt wouldn't have been satisfied in a public place. My only hope was that Ashton wasn't going to keep me waiting much longer for that kiss I'd dreamt of for the last two years.

The ride home was quiet. He held my hand, his thumb moving back and forth across the top of mine. My insides were liquid. My thighs quivered with desire.

The spa had rid me of every last bit of body hair, and I was damn glad of that. I prayed that Ashton would kiss every last inch of me with slow, burning kisses.

And even as I thought about what I wanted him to do to me, I still had no idea if he had any plans to do such a thing.

I didn't want to push him. But my God, how I wanted him to take me like he owned me.

When the car pulled up in front of my apartment building, I

broke out into a sweat. I crossed my fingers by my side. "You're coming up, right?"

He nodded as the driver came to open the door for us to get out. "I don't want you walking up to your apartment alone, baby."

My heart sped up as he called me baby again. I loved hearing him call me that. I wanted to hear him say it many more times—I wanted to hear him whisper it in my ear as he took me.

Even as we headed up to my place, I still wasn't sure if he would be coming in with me. He had just said he didn't want me to walk alone, was all.

When the elevator doors opened and we headed to my door, I felt my knees going weak. My body was shaking with desire.

He has to come inside with me!

I knew better than to ask him, but I prayed he would ask me if he could.

He held his hand out for my key then opened the door for me. "You're such a gentleman, Ashton."

I saw his Adam's apple bob in his throat as he gulped. "I'm glad you think so." He pulled me into the dark living room but stayed just inside the door.

I could feel my heart pounding in my chest as he put his hands on my shoulders, then moved them to my back to pull me to him. It was so dark, I couldn't see his eyes. But I could feel the energy that flowed between us.

He moved so slowly that I began to wonder if he really was going to do it. But when his lips touched mine, holding me so tightly in his arms, I fell apart. My nails bit into his biceps as I held him back. Then he pushed his tongue through my lips to tangle with mine.

Fireworks went off inside of my head and I lost myself in him in a way I'd had no idea was possible.

CHAPTER TWENTY

Ashton

One kiss just wasn't going to do it for me. Not with her in my arms, finally. With her mouth giving in to mine. With her bedroom only feet away. I wasn't going to deny myself any longer.

I couldn't, even if I had wanted to.

Our hands moved like fire over each other, learning each other's bodies. Somehow, I did have the presence of mind to close and lock the door before she led me to her bedroom.

I wanted to go slow; I really did. But our bodies took over. Her hands pushed and pulled at my clothes and mine did the same to her. All she had left on was the jewelry I had given her. And it looked like sparkling magic as the dim light hit the gold and the diamonds.

Pushing her onto the bed, my mouth ached to kiss every part of her. I started at the bottom, at her little pink toes, and then moved up until my mouth was at her glistening cunt.

When I looked up at her, I found her biting her lip so hard I was afraid she would draw blood if I didn't do something about it. So I kissed her pussy lips, and she made a terrible moan as she arched up. "Yes! God, Yes!"

My fingers dug into the flesh of her creamy thighs as I ran my tongue up and down her hot folds. "Baby ... Baby, you taste so good."

Her hands ran through my hair as I kissed and licked her. My cock was pulsing—it wanted to be inside of her so badly. And when she pulled me up, panting as she said, "Ashton, please, baby. I want you inside of me. Please," well I couldn't resist the urge any longer.

I moved up her body, loving the way our skin felt as my body glided over hers. She pulled her knees up as I settled between her legs.

Grasping her face with one hand so she was looking into my eyes, I used my free one to guide my cock into her. The way her eyes closed as I entered her made my heart sore. "Yes," came her soft word. Her hands gripped my arms tightly. "Oh, God, yes."

"Baby," I murmured as I moved slow and easy, taking in the way her pussy felt around my cock. It had been so damn long. But never had I felt anything like this.

It was meant to be. I knew that without a doubt now.

My head went light, and my body took over. Moving in and out of her sweet cunt, I knew I was home.

It wasn't sex. It was so much more than that. I saw stars; I felt waves flowing through me. It wasn't normal. It was beyond my wildest imagination.

When I kissed my way up her neck, then along her cheek, I felt wetness there. She'd been crying. "Are you okay?" I whispered against her cheek.

Her hands moved up to hold my face between them. "I'm so much more than just okay, Ashton. You have no idea how good I am."

I was glad to hear that. "Good. I am too. This is right. I can feel it. I was wrong to wait so long."

"Never mind that." She pulled me to kiss her then released my lips. "All that matters is that we have each other now."

I had to agree. "That is all that matters." Kissing my way to her ear, I bit her earlobe, then whispered, "I love you."

With a moan, she said, "I love you, too."

With our verbal release came a burst of energy.

She loves me!

I moved faster and harder, taking her body and making her understand that she belonged to me. No one else could ever make her feel the way I could.

Panting and moaning, she moved faster too. Her nails gouged into my back as she rocked her body with mine.

The lovemaking had turned into something else. Our bodies demanded more. I slammed my cock into her, feeling it go even deeper into her. Then I pulled out and turned her over. I wanted to go deeper, and by the way she backed up to me as she got on her hands and knees, I knew she wanted that too.

Grabbing her by the waist, I held her as I slammed back into her. "Yes!" she cried out.

Slapping her ass, I plunged into her over and over with a savage force. This wasn't like me. I had never been this kind of lover. I always tended toward soft and sweet. This was new to me.

But it was a new thing that I liked very much.

Nina brought out things in me I'd had no idea were hidden inside.

The first ripple of her cunt around my cock told me her climax was near, and when her body clamped down on me, I was helpless. I spurted my load into her as we both screamed with the release.

She fell on the bed, and I fell right on top of her as we tried to regain our breath. Thinking I might be squishing her, I rolled off to one side. She immediately came to lie on my chest, kissing it as she mumbled, "I love you so much."

My heart actually hurt, I felt so much love for her. I put my arm around her shoulders then kissed the top of her head. "Me too, baby. Me too."

Pulling her head up after we could breathe normally again, she looked at me. "Wanna take a shower with me? I have to wash this makeup off. I never sleep in it."

"Hell, yes, I do." I got out of bed then picked her up, carrying her naked body across the room.

"Ashton, I have roommates. We can't go out there naked." She jerked her head toward the closet. "Let's grab a couple of robes. Mine isn't going to fit you very well, but it's better than nothing."

As I put her down and waited for her to get us something to put on, I thought about this setup she had at her apartment. And I knew it wasn't going to work out for me.

But it was too soon to ask her for more just yet.

The robe was constricting, to say the least. But it covered enough of me to make me somewhat decent for our stroll to the one bathroom they all shared.

After closing the door and locking it, I pulled the robe off and watched her as she dropped hers.

My cock sprang to life, and I nearly tackled her as she stood with her back to me and started the shower. "Ashton!"

Biting her neck, I lifted her in my arms. "Oh, baby, this shower is going to be fun."

I climbed into the tub with her, then pressed her body against the wall. Pulling her legs up, I had her wrap them around me then I pushed my hard cock back into her.

The way her nails trailed up and down my back made me hot and crazy for her. I couldn't get enough. I finally had her, and it seemed I wasn't about to let her get a wink of sleep.

The warm water ran over us as I fucked her like she was the only woman in the world. She turned me into some kind of a voracious beast who had to have her any way I could get her.

When her nails curled into my back, I got ready for the feeling of her cunt throbbing around my dick. Already, I knew the signs of her body, and when she came, I came too.

We growled and moaned as my cum filled her. My cock throbbed and jerked, sending more cum into her.

And as that settled down, my brain began to work. "Um, I didn't ask this. I wasn't thinking straight, obviously. Are you on any kind of birth control?"

She laughed. "The shot. No reason to be afraid."

"I'm not afraid." I kissed the side of her neck before letting her down. "Just wondering. If you got knocked up, I wouldn't have one problem with that."

She looked at me with a very serious look in her eyes. "You sure about that?"

I nodded, then picked up the bottle of honeysuckle scented shampoo. "I thought you used this scent. And yeah, I'm sure about what I said. Now that I have you, I have no intentions of ever letting you go, just so you know. And so you know this too, you are officially off the market."

"Oh, am I?" she asked with a giggle.

I poured some shampoo into my palm then lathered it into her hair. "You are. No more men for you, my sweet thing. Only me from now on."

"Well, aren't you sure of yourself," she said with a smile, then winked at me. "But you have every right to be. And just so you know, you're off the market now too."

"I've been off the market." I moved her head back to rinse her hair.

When I pulled her head back up, I saw her eyes were glistening. "Is this really happening, Ashton?"

With a kiss to her swollen lips, I let her know it was real. "I love you, Nina Kramer. I think I have for a long time now."

She sighed then laid her head on my chest. "Me too."

Internally, I began to berate myself for waiting so damn long. I had been a fool. But then she ran her hands up my arms, as if sensing what I was doing. "The time was finally right. I'm glad we waited. Really knowing you, learning more about you as your friend before anything else, that makes this special."

Laughing, I had to say, "Girl, you really can read my mind." I kissed her again, loving the fact that I could kiss her whenever I wanted to now.

She pulled away from me as I pawed at her. "I need to wash your hair now."

Being almost a foot taller than her, I gave her a quizzical look. "And just how are you going to do that, may I ask?"

She turned off the shower and put the plug into the bottom of the tub. "In the bath, of course."

We settled into the tub, me in front of her. She made me lean back on her plump tits as she washed my hair. I had never felt so comfortable. The way her hands moved over me soothed me in a way I didn't know was possible.

"I could get used to this, baby."

She ran her soapy hands over my chest. "Me too."

Taking her hand, I pulled it up and kissed it. Then I turned around and pulled her legs down. "I can't seem to keep this cock of mine from getting hard."

"Lucky me," she said with a grin.

"I don't know how we're going get along at work." I pushed my cock into her tight pussy again.

"We'll just have to be discreet." She moved her legs to accommodate me.

The thought of her bent over my desk in my office sprang into my mind again. "And quiet, too." I moved with slow thrusts, so we didn't make too much of a mess with the water.

Already plans had begun to hatch in my head. The future lay in front of us. And it looked bright.

CHAPTER TWENTY-ONE

Nina

My eyelids were heavy as I began to wake up. A leg was thrown over mine; an arm lay on my side. And warm breath moved steadily across the back of my neck.

It's real!

The night before had been so fantastic that I was sure it had to have been a dream. But feeling Ashton lying behind me, holding me, that wasn't a dream at all.

This is real!

I didn't open my eyes. I lay perfectly still, loving every second of the way it felt. His skin touching mine, his body against my back, even the way he breathed captivated me.

I could live like this forever.

In bed, with Ashton wrapped around me, that was a place I never wanted to leave. And I wouldn't have, either, except for the fact that my bladder was full and it was beginning to get uncomfortable.

Easing his arm off me, then his leg, I sat up, rubbing my eyes with the back of my hand. When I stood up, I found my body aching in the best possible way. Stiff and sore, I made my way to the bathroom, making sure to grab a robe to cover myself before I left my bedroom.

In the bathroom mirror, I found my hair a mess, but my face had a glow about it. "Man, he sure has done a number on you, sis." My cheeks were red from his whiskers, my lips swollen from his kisses.

When I sat on the toilet, I saw that the insides of my thighs were also red, again from his whiskered cheeks. A smile curved my lips. But it went away just as quickly when I felt the burning sensation as I peed. "Ow!"

But the smile crept back as I recalled just why that burn was there, and suddenly I didn't mind the pain at all. Sure, my body hurt all over, but that was because of the strenuous workout Ashton had given me. An immensely pleasurable workout.

After washing my face, brushing my teeth, taming my hair, and dousing myself with a bit of lavender body spray, I felt fit to get back to bed. Cuddling with Ashton sounded like heaven to me.

When I got back into my room, I found Ashton sitting up. His eyes were on me. "I missed you."

"I wasn't gone but a few minutes." I pulled the robe off, tossing it to the side. Strolling over to him, I added an extra sway to my step, flaunting my body.

His hands met my hips, holding me still. "Let me look at you." His lips pressed against my stomach, then he ran his tongue around my belly button.

It sent chills through me. I ran my hands through his blond waves, which had fallen out of the man-bun he'd had it in during the night. Now it was loose, and I wanted nothing more than to tangle my hands in it.

Just as I was falling into the abyss that was Ashton, a loud bang came on the wall. Then muffled voices came through it, cursing and laughing. "That's Sandy's room."

The sound of not one, but two male voices laughing had Ashton looking at me with one raised brow. "She's got two boyfriends?"

I shook my head. "She has no boyfriends. She refuses to be

monogamous. But this is the first time I've heard two guys with her at the same time."

"Me first!" one of the guys shouted.

"Boys, no need to fight. One can take the top, and one can take the bottom," Sandy offered them.

I was so embarrassed, my entire body heated up. "Oh, God. Ashton, I'm so sorry."

With a smile, he pulled me down on top of him. "Don't be. Just come here, and we can make some noise of our own. Forget about them. I already have."

He turned over with me, pinning me underneath him. His cerulean eyes gazed into mine as I brushed his long hair back. "It's nice to see you in my bed this morning, Ashton."

"It's nice to be in your bed this morning, Nina." He kissed the tip of my nose. "I hope you know I plan to monopolize your time this weekend."

"I hope you know that makes me very happy." I ran my hands over his broad shoulders and bit my lip as his muscles rippled.

Nuzzling my neck, he whispered, "I had better go wash up a bit."

I hated to let him go. But I had to. "Go and wash up. I'll be right here when you get back."

With a swift kiss to my cheek, he climbed off me then walked away. I turned to my side to watch him. His ass was chiseled and magnificent. His shoulders were wide, and the muscles in his back moved with each step he took. Along the back of one shoulder, there was an eagle with its wings spread, as if it was flying.

I never knew that Ashton sported any ink. There were still a lot of things to learn about this man I'd thought I knew pretty damn well.

After putting on one of my robes, he slipped out of my room, and I closed my eyes. I couldn't ever recall being as happy as I was then. My heart beat with a steady rhythm. I felt perky even though I'd had little sleep.

This has to be love.

There wasn't anything else to which I could attribute this feeling of well-being.

I am in love with Ashton Lange.

I had never mentioned love, or even thought about it during the past two years of knowing the man. But with that first kiss, I knew I was in love with him. I'd fallen in love through the years and hadn't even realized it.

As I lay there, I let myself dream of the future. I was sure he would want to move things along fast, now that we were open about things. But how fast did I want to move?

I wasn't sure about that. I still had some worries about how Ashton would take things. I wasn't some fool who thought his issues with his past would just disappear with our new relationship.

I did hope that the issues would slowly dissipate. And now that he was seeing a therapist, my hopes were higher than I ever thought they would be.

We could make a future together; I knew we could. And I knew it wouldn't always be the rosiest of pictures. But I was ready for it all. Whatever came with the man, I would take it.

When my door opened, I found Ashton striding in, red-faced. "I met one of your roomie's friends."

"Oh, hell!" I sat up, the blanket falling off my breasts as I did.

He looked directly at them. "Um, yeah." He pulled off the robe but went for his clothes, which were strewn around. "We should go to my place."

"But it's so early." I stretched then patted the bed. "Come on, let's stay here for a little while longer then we can go if you want to."

"I want to go now." He pulled on his underwear. "That guy told me there are a few more people coming to join them. Apparently, it's orgy Saturday here at your casa, baby." He looked at me with an odd expression. "Is this something you were aware of?"

I laughed. "No. I'm sure that guy was just kidding." I patted the bed again to encourage him to climb back in with me.

"I don't know." He shook his head as he picked his pants up off the floor. "He said we should come and join them. He seemed pretty serious. I would just feel better if we left." He pulled on his pants as he gave me a stern look. "And you're coming too. Don't you think for half a second that I'm leaving you here. Get up, girl. We're out of here."

I laughed as I got up. It was obvious that Ashton was set on leaving. And I liked the fact that he was adamant that I come with him.

He always had looked out for me. I expected that would only grow with our budding relationship. "Okay, Daddy."

"Daddy?" he asked, as he stopped putting his clothes on for a second. "I think I like that."

Giggling, I went up to him, wrapping my arms around his neck. "Carry me, Daddy."

He picked me up and I kissed him as I ran my legs around him. My pussy pulsed against his now covered cock. I wanted him so bad, I couldn't control my movements.

But then some loud grunting crept through the wall, followed by a shrill, screaming moan by Sandy, and I was ready to go too.

He put me down and scowled at me. "Let's get the hell out of here before we hear things that will haunt us."

I had no idea what had gotten into Sandy, but I didn't want to be any part of it. I supposed that Kyle's absence for the weekend had spurred her into making some naughty plans.

Just as I was thinking about what I should do if her bender was going to be happening all weekend, Ashton said, "Pack a bag. You're staying with me all weekend. You can come back here after work on Monday."

I wasn't used to being told what to do, but I liked it. "Okay."

After packing a bag and getting dressed, we headed down to catch a cab to his apartment. He held my hand, running his thumb over the top of it as he went from looking out the window to looking at me. "We can make breakfast together at my place. I've got some eggs and bacon."

"Good. I'll make the eggs, you make the bacon, and we'll be eating in no time." I leaned in to kiss his cheek. And then it just came out again. "I love you."

His crooked smile had me smiling right back. "I love you too." His lips pressed against the top of my head. "More than I knew was possible."

My heart skipped a beat. *Does that mean he loves me more than he loved Natalia?*

I didn't dare ask. But I did wonder if that's what he meant.

Cuddling up to his side, I whispered, "I feel more for you than I've ever felt for anyone."

His hand cupped my chin as he placed his lips on mine. The touch was so gentle that it made my body all fluttery. My stomach filled with butterflies. My head went light.

He made a long, deep sigh as he pulled back. "This is going to be a piece of cake."

I wasn't sure what he meant. "What is?"

"Loving you." His eyes sparkled as he looked into mine. "I've fought this for what seems like forever. I was so afraid that transitioning from friends to lovers would be awkward at best. But nothing we do feels awkward. It all feels so natural. Like we've been doing this for a very long time."

The way he was looking into my eyes had me thinking he wanted to tell me more, but he wasn't sure how to word it. So I took a guess, hoping he'd be more willing to share if he wasn't the one to bring it up. "It feels different with me, doesn't it?"

He nodded. "It does."

Since he hadn't balked at that, I went a bit further. "It feels more natural, huh?"

"It does." His hand moved up my arm then his fingertips grazed my jawline. "I have no doubts about you, Nina. Now that I've let go, I'm all in. I've never been all in before. Not the way I am with you."

My heart raced with the knowledge that I wouldn't be living in a dead girl's shadow. I had his heart, and that was all that mattered to me, because he had my heart too.

CHAPTER TWENTY-TWO

Ashton

Monday came, leaving the weekend behind in a blur of sheets, showers, and a few intense meals that I would never forget. Eating cheeses and meats off Nina's tummy was better than any cheeseboard I'd ever been served.

But the work week interrupted our little party for two, separating us for the duration of the long day. Separating us for small amounts of time, anyway.

Popping into her office, I found her finishing up with the social media work she did for Lila. "Hey."

Her green eyes fluttered away from the computer screen to look at me. "Hey, you."

Closing the door behind me, I went straight to her, picking her up, then setting her on the small desk. I couldn't hold back; I had to kiss her.

After a good long kiss, I pulled my mouth away then rested my forehead against hers. "I've never been happier that we work together. At least I get a little taste of you now and then, since we're in the same building."

Her fingers traced circles on my back. "Me too." She moved in for another kiss and I obliged her.

When our lips parted, I sighed. "Baby, I've got it bad for you."

She laughed, a light sound that echoed in my heart. "Me too, babe. It's coffee time in Lila's office. I'll bring you back a big mug of it. I'm so excited to tell them our big news."

I couldn't have wiped the smile off my face if I'd tried. Slapping her ass as she walked away from me, I said, "Don't tell them all the details. We have to keep a few secrets."

She turned to me, her finger to her lips in a shushing gesture. "Not to worry. No one will ever know how much I like it when you …"

I stopped her. "Hush, now. The walls have ears, you know."

Opening the door, she laughed as she walked out of her office. I followed her out, going up to see Artimus. We shared the elevator ride up. Her hand took mine as we moved back to let more people in. I loved the way her hand felt in mine.

It was insane how my heart swelled with love for her at her every touch. I knew it was a short amount of time, in some people's eyes. But our love had been quietly growing for the past two years, whether we'd realized it or not. It made perfect sense to me.

We were alone as we rode up the last few floors, and I took the chance to get in one last kiss before we had to part ways. "Miss me," I told her before the elevator doors opened and we were in the penthouse lobby.

Blowing me a kiss, she headed down the hallway as I went to Artimus' office. All the while, Brady and Veronica gave us blank stares.

I looked at them over my shoulder, "Yeah, we're a thing now."

Brady cleared his throat. "Us too."

I stopped and turned to look at them. "Really?" I was just kidding. Everyone knew about their custodial closet escapades.

Veronica nodded. "We moved in together last week."

"Well, you guys are more serious than anyone realized." I jerked my head toward what was known as their closet. "We all thought it was just a casual work affair you guys were having. Congratulations, then. I wish you both all the best."

Veronica was staring at the closet and didn't say a word. But Brady was quick to accept my congratulations, "Thanks, Ashton. Congrats to you and Nina too."

"Thanks." I knocked on Artimus' door. "It's me. Ashton."

When the door opened, I saw Duke was also visiting our boss. "There he is."

I went to take a seat on the sofa opposite them. "Here I am. And have I got some news for you guys."

Artimus smiled at me. "The date went well, then?"

"Better than well." I crossed my legs, holding one ankle as I thought back on the flurry of passion that had been my weekend.

Duke broke into deep laughter. "Sounds like someone got laid."

I shook my head. "It was way more than just that, Duke. So much more than that."

Artimus seemed surprised. "More than that? So just what did you two get up to on Friday night?"

"We went out and had a great dinner. Had some awesome conversations. And in the end, I walked her up to her apartment. I kissed her goodnight." I sighed without meaning to.

Duke laughed again. "Your first kiss, right?"

"It was." I could feel the tingle on my tongue the same way I had when I first kissed her.

Artimus pushed for more information. "And then you left?"

Shaking my head, I went on, "No. I did not leave just then."

Duke howled like a wolf. "The dry spell is over. He's finally gotten some rain."

Artimus punched Duke in the arm. "Rogue!" He looked at me. "Never mind him. You know how athletes are. Did you stay the night with her?"

"I did." My chest swelled with pride. "And the next morning, I took her home with me. Where I kept her until this very morning. We rode to work together."

"Are you moving her in already?" Duke asked me with a surprised expression.

"Not yet." My fingers tapped on top of my thigh as I thought about that. "But I want to move her in as soon as possible."

"I don't know," Artimus mused, his hand moving over his chin. "I wouldn't go rushing anything, Ashton. At the very least, confer with Dr. Patel on how you should take things. You don't want to rush into things, then suffer a relapse."

I didn't like the way he talked about my grieving issues. "Artimus, I don't have cancer. I've got some issues, but nothing more than that."

"Still, don't rush," he cautioned me. "I know you two have waited a long time for this, but don't make the mistake of moving too fast."

I felt like it was far too late to stop the rollercoaster we had gotten on. "Easier said than done."

Duke nodded. "Yeah, I know." He punched Artimus in the arm. "You and I didn't exactly follow that advice, Artimus. And we turned out just fine."

With a stoic stare, Artimus informed him, "We also didn't have the past that he has." He looked at me. "Go slow, Ashton. Be cautious. I would hate for either you or Nina to get hurt because you rushed things."

"I'll try, Artimus. I will. But where she's concerned, it doesn't seem possible." I thought back to how I'd imagined our first time would be. "I had this plan to make our first time special. I was going to go very slowly, take my time, you know."

Duke laughed. "Bet you didn't take your time at all!"

Shaking my head, I confessed, "No, I did not take my time at all." Going further into the weekend, I added, "And I never thought I would be asking her to stay the weekend with me so soon either. But when her roommate decided to have a little sexy weekend of her own —with more than a few guests in attendance—I didn't ask Nina to come home with me; I demanded she do so."

"Her roommate did what?" Artimus asked.

My eyes trained on his to gauge his reaction. "She had an orgy."

Duke guffawed. "No way!"

"I swear." My hands went into the air. "We heard her in her room with two guys. Then I went to the bathroom, and there was one of them, standing in the hallway wearing nothing more than what looked like her panties to cover himself. He invited us to their orgy. So, I told Nina we were out of there."

Duke and Artimus looked at me with stunned expressions. Then Artimus said, "Don't let that be the reason you ask her to move in with you, Ashton."

"Oh, that will be part of the reason I ask her to move in with me—I don't want her living in a place that makes her uncomfortable. But the biggest part will be because I doubt I'll be able to sleep well without her." I scratched my head as I thought about how I would get by tonight. "I know it's only been three nights, but I'm pretty sure I'm already addicted to holding her all night long."

Duke got up and went to get something out of the fridge. "Okay, Artimus. It's time to make some bets here. I give Romeo here one month before he asks her to marry him."

"I'm not that impulsive, Duke. Give me some credit," but even as I said the words, flashes of engagement rings went through my mind.

Artimus' expression was stern. "I'm serious, Ashton. Don't jump into anything permanent."

I had been alone for so long. More alone than most, I would wager, having lived with the memory of Natalia for so long. And now I had Nina. I didn't want to be alone anymore. But I knew Artimus was right. I had to slow down. "I'll try my hardest to slow things down. She'll be staying at her place this week. And maybe I'll see if I can get through next weekend without her by my side." I shook my head. "No. Why would I do that to myself? Artimus, I've been alone for so long. Why deny myself now?"

"I'm not saying to deny yourself. I'm just saying to keep the words 'move in with me' and 'marry me' out of your mouth for a while. That's all I'm saying." He looked at Duke, who was staring into the fridge. "Can you grab me an apple juice, Duke?"

"Sure." Duke looked at me. "You want anything?"

"Nah. Nina's making coffee in Lila's office. She'll be bringing me one soon." With a deep breath, I tried to slow my train of thought. It was barreling in Nina's direction and seemed unable to stop.

Artimus asked Duke, "Why don't you drink that coffee, Duke? It's amazing."

"I don't do caffeine." He tossed a bottle of apple juice to Artimus, then opened a bottle of water for himself. "You've never noticed that?"

I shook my head. "I haven't noticed that."

"Me neither." Artimus took a long drink of the juice. "Is there any reason that you don't do caffeine?"

"It makes me nervous. I hate to be nervous." He downed the water. "I'm going to go to the gym. Anyone want to join me?"

"I could use a workout." I got up to follow him.

Artimus nodded and got up too. "That sounds like a great idea. The gym, a little coffee, and in a little while, we'll do lunch. Sounds like our typical day."

And he was right. That was our typical day. We pushed each other in the best of ways.

I knew those guys had my back. I knew they weren't telling me to slow my roll with Nina out of anything but concern for my best interests.

As we got on the elevator, I bumped shoulders with Artimus. "Thanks again for not listening to me and setting me up with Dr. Patel."

"That's what friends are for, Ashton. We do shit even when our friends complain and tell us not to." He bumped my shoulder back. "And I want you to know that I'm here for you. Don't let anything get stuck in your craw again. Do you hear me?"

I had kept so much to myself for so long, but he was right; I did need to be open with him and Duke. "I promise." And then my mind was back on Nina. "We've already said the L word to each other. And I should confess this to you guys: I love her more than I've ever loved anyone."

"You know that already?" Duke asked with wide eyes.

"I do." I was sure I loved her more than anything.

Artimus made a tsk sound. "Well, taking things slow certainly looks like it will be next to impossible for these two."

I thought so too.

CHAPTER TWENTY-THREE

Nina

Thursday night, my cell in my hand and my head on the pillow, I lay in bed talking to Ashton on the phone. "I miss you too."

Even though we saw each other at work each day, it was hard to walk away from each other to go our separate ways once the workday ended.

"Please reconsider Saturday, baby," he asked me again.

He'd asked me to come spend at least Saturday night with him. And I did want to, but Lila and Julia had cautioned me about moving too fast with him. And I felt like they were right. "I don't know, Ashton."

"I'll make it worth your while, Nina. I've got some chocolate ice cream, cherries, and whipped cream. I can make a Nina sundae," he tempted me.

"That does sound good." Who was I kidding? That sounded amazing.

It was so hard to keep going slow after all this time. "Close your eyes and imagine me licking chocolate of you as it drips down your stomach to your ripe peach ..."

"Ashton!" I groaned, knowing exactly what he was trying to do, but already wet with desire and helpless to resist his little tricks.

"Come on, baby. Tell Daddy what he wants to hear." He made a deep growl that sent me over the edge.

"Okay!" I sat up in bed as excitement filled me. "Yes, I'll spend Saturday night with you."

With a deep chuckle, he asked, "How about Friday and Sunday nights too then?"

"I would. I really would. But I've got to get laundry done on Sunday. And Friday, I've got an appointment at the dentist to get my teeth cleaned. I'm leaving work early tomorrow to make that appointment. But Saturday, I'll come to you." I was already thinking about all the things we could do, and getting hot and bothered just at the thought.

"I'll take what I can get," he said. "I love you, girl."

The words were new, but I knew they would never get old. "I love you too, Ashton."

Working only a half-day on Friday, Ashton proved hard to let go of as he kissed me goodbye in his office. I noticed that his usually cluttered desk was cleared of every last thing. And when he pushed me up against it, I had the feeling he wanted to get a little nasty in his office.

"I've got to get going. I've got that appointment," I reminded him.

"Your teeth look great already." His mouth took mine again before he let up. "Skip the appointment."

I could feel his cock as it pulsed against my aching core. "I would, but he'll charge me anyway. I've got to go, babe."

His hands moved up my back, grasping me behind the head as he held me tight. "I'm trying to take it slow with you, Nina, but it's a losing battle. I think about you nonstop. I wake up and find myself wrapped around the pillows, wishing it was you. And when I realize you're not there, I can hardly go back to sleep. I love you. I miss you."

"Me too." I wasn't lying. I did miss him like crazy. And I understood his struggle all too well with this going slow thing. "Talk to Dr.

Patel. See what she thinks about things. And take her advice, Ashton. Whatever it is. I've got to go."

His hands held mine tight. "Go to my place after the appointment." He reached into his pocket and pulled out a key, placing it in my palm. "Please, stay this weekend with me. I don't want to wait until tomorrow. I don't want you to leave me on Sunday. Stay with me until Monday. Please, baby. You have no idea how hard this is for me."

"My laundry, though," I reminded him.

With a huff, he said, "Do it when you go to your place to pack your bags, or bring it with you." He smiled at me, thinking he'd solved everything. Then he kissed the tip of my nose. "And I'll bring dinner home tonight. And you'll be there waiting for me. It'll be like a dream come true for me."

Who was I to squash his dreams? "K."

And with that one word, I earned another soul-shattering kiss.

The rest of the day went by slowly. The dental appointment took forever. The laundry took forever, plus some. And then I had to pack and catch a cab to his place.

Letting myself into his apartment felt a little odd. I looked around as I walked in. It would be another two hours before Ashton got home. I had no idea what I would do with my time.

Then I got a call from him. "Hi, babe."

"You home yet?" he asked me.

"I'm at your place, yes." I smiled at his slip up. I looked around. I could see myself easily making the place our home.

"Good. Take a hot bath and have a glass of wine. You should be done about the same time that I get home. I'm bringing Chinese," he told me.

"Yum. Don't forget ..."

He interrupted me, "The eggrolls. Not to worry. I do know what you like, baby."

And he did, too. We'd eaten so many meals together; he knew what I liked just as well as I did. And I knew what he liked too.

It was great already knowing the man I'd fallen in love with so well.

"Okay, I'll take a bath then."

"And put on one of my T-shirts. I've been fantasizing about coming home to find you wearing one of them all day long. And leave the panties off," he added.

"Feeling randy, baby?" I asked with a giggle.

"Very. See you soon. Get all fresh for Daddy."

"Bye, you freak." I ended the call and laughed all the way to the kitchen.

His apartment was way nicer than the one I lived in. It was roomier and had state of the art appliances. The flooring and countertops were all top of the line too.

I had the feeling that he would be asking me to move in before too long. And I wasn't sure what I would do if he did.

As I sipped the wine and soaked up the hot, sudsy water, I let my mind wander to that thought and linger.

My roommates would have to find someone else to move in. They couldn't afford the rent on their own. But I was pretty sure Sandy could find someone. She knew lots of people.

But I didn't want to live off of Ashton. Perhaps I could offer to pay half the bills. That would be fair, and keep me from feeling like I was being taken care of.

As I lay there in the hot water, I looked around the place and thought I could definitely call it home. And then my cell rang, and I had to end my little dream to get out of the tub.

It was Ashton again. "Yes?"

"I need you to come unlock the door. I gave you my key. I've been ringing the bell, but I guess you didn't hear it," he said.

"Damn! I'll go do that right now." I put the phone down and grabbed a towel, wrapping it around me as I ran to open the door.

Just as I swung it open, one of his neighbors passed by behind him. He stopped and didn't even try to hide the fact that he was taking me all in. My eyes went wide as saucers as I stepped back to hide myself from the stranger.

Thank goodness Ashton was oblivious to the man, walking in with a smile on his face. "Hey, baby."

I closed the door in the other man's face and locked it, trying to ignore the fact that I'd just been leered at by a stranger. "I'll run and get changed."

"That's okay." He put the bag of Chinese food on the coffee table, then picked me up in his arms, letting the towel fall away from my body. "I'm hungry for you anyway."

His teeth grazed my neck as he carried me straight to his room. "Are you serious?"

"Very." He tossed me on the bed, then disrobed in no time. His cock was at attention, ready to go. But then he stopped and raised one brow. "Wait. Are you hungry?"

I got on my hands and knees, wiggling my finger at him as my mouth watered. "I am. Come here."

The sexy grin that spread over his face only made me hotter for him. He came to me, placing his hands on my shoulders. "Do I have something you'd like?"

"You do." I licked my lips as I took his cock into my hands, running them up and down the long length. "Can I eat until I'm full?" I looked up at him to get my answer.

When I'd given him head, he didn't want to come in my mouth, preferring to come in my pussy, he'd said. That's why I asked. When he nodded, I made a little joyful squeal, then kissed the tip of his cock.

"Damn, baby. Go for it." He stroked my hair as I moved my mouth over his penis. Then he made a groan that instantly made me wet.

Moving my mouth up and down his cock, I sucked gently and ran my tongue along the underside. Using my hands, I made sure to stimulate every part of his organ.

He moved his hips, helping me to take him at the speed he needed. The way he moaned sent chills through my body, and when the first bit of precum hit my tongue, I went down on him with a ravenous hunger.

"Ah!" he yelled as he spurted down my throat. "Shit!"

The salty taste of his cum satisfied my craving. But I wasn't the only one who needed satisfying. He pushed me back, then kissed my cunt before licking my folds with his hot, wet tongue.

Putting his hands on my tits, he squeezed them as he ate me. My body felt completely connected, like it was one pulsing organ. Everything was heightened. His mouth moved on me like he knew every nook and cranny, and just what to do to make things tick inside of me.

Arching up to make his tongue go deeper into my pussy, I cried out as I came. "Fuck!"

Licking up everything he'd made me give him, he growled like a hungry wolf. Then he pulled his head away from me, wiping his mouth with the back of his hand. "On your belly."

I flipped to my stomach and he moved his body on top of mine. His dick went into me as he kissed the back of my neck.

Purring like a kitten, I loved the way his skin felt as he moved his body along my back. No one had ever taken me that way before. It felt even more intimate than missionary style.

He didn't even try to keep his weight off me. I could feel his entire body moving as he pushed his cock into me deeper than he could in any other position.

His lips touched the shell of my ear. "I love you so much, baby. You've got no idea how much."

One of his hands moved along my arm, pulling my hand up. Our fingers laced together, making our connection even better somehow. "I love you more than you can understand," I let him know as I pushed my body up against him, demanding everything he could give me.

His mouth moved over my neck, sending shivers through me. He licked up one side of my neck, then bit my earlobe. "I'm not letting you out of my bed this whole weekend, baby."

"Promise?"

CHAPTER TWENTY-FOUR

Ashton

Feeding Nina cold Chinese food in bed wasn't going to cut it for me. She had to get something hot to eat, even though she protested that cold food would be just fine with her.

So, at three o'clock in the morning, I ordered us a veggie pizza with extra cheese. "Yeah, fifteen minutes is more than fine, thanks." I put the phone down and looked at Nina, who had gotten out of bed and was traipsing toward the bathroom. "What do you want to drink, baby?"

"A glass of cold milk, if you have any," she said, then went into the bathroom, closing the door behind her.

Getting off the bed, I put on some pajamas then went to the kitchen to get the drinks and get out some paper plates and napkins. I thought a picnic in bed sounded good.

Then she came into the living room, wearing one of my T-shirts and nothing else, making my dick go hard again. "Oh, shit." I looked down and watched my PJ bottoms tent.

She pointed at my erection and put her hand over her mouth as she giggled. "Did I do that?"

Putting everything I'd gathered back down on the countertop, I went to her, taking her up in my arms. "Is there anything about you that won't set my cock off?"

She shrugged, and we both laughed as I twirled her around. I could not get enough of the woman, that was for sure. We wrestled around until a knock came at the door. "Pizza's here." I let her go to answer the door.

She ducked into the kitchen so that she wouldn't be seen in the short shirt. "I'll pour the milk. Do you want a glass too?"

"Yep." I opened the door, taking the pizza and tipping the delivery guy. "Thanks, man."

He looked at the ten I'd given him and smiled. "Thank you!"

Taking our pie, I headed toward the bedroom. "Come on, baby."

"Ashton, get your butt back here. We are not eating in the bedroom. Are you crazy?" She placed the glasses of milk on the table, then put the paper plates down too. "We aren't barbarians, you know."

"Eating pizza in bed is barbaric?" I had to ask, as I'd had no idea there were any such rules in my house.

She pulled out a chair and took a seat. "Yes, it is. My mother never let us have anything more than a glass of water in our bedrooms. If you leave food or sugary drinks lying around, then you'll get bugs in your house. You don't want bugs in your house, do you?"

I guess I didn't want bugs in my house, because I took the pizza to the table and sat down. "I've never thought about that."

She gave me a cynical look. "Do you eat in your bedroom often?"

"Nope. This was going to be the first time, actually." I did have a plan in mind. And then I remembered eating some cheese and meat off her tummy the last time we were together. "And what about eating in your bedroom at your apartment, Nina?"

She looked away, as if she'd been caught in some lie. "Oh, over there doesn't matter. Kyle and Sandy take all kinds of crap to their rooms. We have to spray for bugs every week to keep them out. But here, well, this place is nice. Too nice to be eating food wherever you feel like it."

"So, no Nina sundae in bed then?" I asked with a frown.

She shook her head, then jerked it toward the kitchen. "But in there is fine."

The sexy grin she gave me had me laughing as she put pieces of pizza on both our plates. "Okay, I see how things are now. You're making rules. I like it."

Her head ducked, then she cut her eyes at me with a shy look in them. "I didn't think about it like that. I just didn't want your place getting messed up. It's a very nice apartment. It should be treated that way."

I took her hand in mine and decided to make up a rule of my own. "How about we start our own little thing right now?"

She looked at our hands. "Like what?"

"I'm not particularly religious, but I would like to start some type of a tradition that we do at each meal. In my mind, it's the many meals we've shared that have brought us so close." It was true. She and I had started out our friendship by joining each other and the others for lunch most days.

"I think that sounds nice." She leaned over and kissed my cheek. "How about we say something that shows how much we appreciate good food and good company?"

"I like that idea." I thought a moment then came up with something. "I'd like to thank the Lord above for this great grub and for this woman's love. Amen." I laughed a little. "What do you think about that?"

"Above and love rhyme." She shook her head. "But grub? I dunno about that word."

"You give it a try." I munched on some pizza while she mulled it over. A minute passed, and she had yet to say a word as she ate too. "See, it's not so easy, is it?"

"No, it's really not." With a shrug, she conceded, "You win, then."

The victory sat well with me. "So, no food in the bedroom, that's your rule. And my rule is a little prayer before we eat. I like this rule-making thing. We should make some more."

She raised her hand like she was in school or something. "Oh! I've got one."

"Shoot." I took a drink of milk as I waited for her new rule.

"We should always put the toilet seat down." She nodded. "That's a good one."

"I don't see why we should do that," I said in confusion.

"Well, I've noticed that you tend to leave the seat up," she told me as she fidgeted a little in her chair. "And if I get up in the middle of the night and I don't want to turn on the light, then I might fall in and get my butt wet."

Now it made sense. "I get it. Okay, we will both completely close the toilet lid then."

She seemed grateful. "Thank you. It will save me some shocking moments if we can do that."

"I'm sure it will." I came up with a great new rule. "And here's the next rule. We both sleep in the buff every night."

She nodded in agreement. "Every night that we're together, we can sleep naked, if you want to. That one's cool with me."

How badly I wanted to tell her that I wanted us to sleep together every night. But Dr. Patel had told me not to rush moving in together. I had just begun my therapy, after all.

That didn't seem to matter to me as much as it mattered to everyone else. I felt this overwhelming need to get Nina into my life —full-time and fast. But I didn't want things to devolve because of my impatient nature.

Time is important, the good doctor had told me. *You need time to grieve, time to free yourself from the guilt you've built up over the years.*

And I needed time to take Nina into my heart properly, a heart that had been closed off until recently.

The funny thing was that I didn't think I needed time to let Nina into my heart. I'd told Dr. Patel that. But she only shook her head, as if she knew me better than I knew myself.

And as far as the grief was going, I wasn't feeling it so sharply anymore. I had more joy in my heart than I could ever recall having.

The guilt? Well, that was still there. I didn't think it would ever go away. But I felt like if the doctor could get over her role in the death of her baby, then I would eventually come to terms with my part in Natalia's early demise.

"You're lost in thought, Ashton," Nina's voice drew me back out.

There was a piece of pizza in one hand and the glass of milk in the other. I had zoned out. "I was just thinking."

"About?" she asked, as she gently moved my hand with the milk onto the table. "You should probably put this down before you spill it."

I didn't want to tell her what I was thinking about. "It's nothing."

"It's something." She put down the pizza and took hold of my hand, drawing it to her heart as she looked into my eyes. "Tell me."

"Dr. Patel has told me that I should take things nice and slow with you." I watched her as she nodded. "You agree?"

"I want things to move forward. And I want them to move fast. But I know that it's not the right thing for either of us. Only a couple of weeks ago, you were guarding your heart and your memory of Natalia. Now, just because we've shared ourselves, you and I both think we can just hurry up and move things forward. But we can't. We can't, because it's not good for you."

I hated feeling like there was something wrong with me. "I'm not sick, Nina. I've got some issues, and I'm dealing with them. And I love you so damn much, and I know that's helping me a lot." I did believe that, even though Dr. Patel had only shaken her head when I'd told her that.

The way Nina's eyes went to an even softer state made my heart melt. She reached out to stroke my bearded cheek. "Aw, Ashton, that's the sweetest thing I've ever heard."

I took her hand, holding it tight. "Nina, what if they're all wrong? What if we don't have to wait? Why do we have to wait for what other people consider to be the right amount of time? No one seems to be taking into account all the time that we've been friends, close friends."

Her lower lip pouted as she thought about what I'd said. "But the doctor is a professional. I'm sure she's seen cases like yours before. She must know what's best for you."

"What about me? Don't I know what's right for me?" I asked her in earnest.

She rolled her lips together as if mustering up some courage to tell me something she knew I wouldn't like. "Look, I know you're a smart man."

"Why do I feel a 'but' coming?" I ran my thumb over her knuckles as my stomach tightened with nerves.

"But," she nodded at me, "you weren't the one who sought professional help. You were thinking you could deal with things on your own. And that wasn't working out very well."

And she was right.

I had gone off the deep end, and I hadn't swum back on my own. I'd had to be saved. Artimus had saved me by throwing me a life preserver in the form of Dr. Patel.

"I'll follow her advice," I admitted in defeat.

Nina got up and came around behind me, running her hand along my shoulders as she did. "Good. I'm with you all the way, babe. So, how about we get back to making crazy love for the rest of this weekend before we have to get back to the grind on Monday?"

Getting up, I let her lead me to the bedroom. "I like the way you think." I tried to get into the moment and tried to stop thinking about the future.

For now, I had Nina. I had her all weekend long, and that was the only thing I needed to be thinking about right then.

The future would be there when we got to it.

CHAPTER TWENTY-FIVE

Nina

A month passed with Ashton and me spending every weekend together. Three nights out of every week, we stayed together. And things were blossoming just fine.

Sundays were the days he took the hardest. We even got into a little spat about how he would start in early on Sunday morning, asking me if I could just stay Monday night too. *Just one more night,* that was always his plea throughout the day.

The sun woke me up as it streamed through his window. Sunday had come, and I was ready for the onset of reasons why one more night wouldn't hurt.

But when I turned over, I found he wasn't even in bed. Sitting up, I looked to find the bathroom door wide open and not a sound of anyone in there either.

Getting up, I picked up a towel off the floor and wrapped it around myself. I went to the living room and found he wasn't in the apartment at all. It was seven in the morning.

Where the hell could he be?

I went back into the bedroom to get my cell to call him. That's when I noticed that I had slept through a text he'd sent me an hour earlier.

-Went to get some things. Be back soon-

With no idea what he'd need to get a seven in the morning on a Sunday, I set about taking a shower and getting ready for the day. We'd started taking outings on Sundays, calling them our fun days.

After getting dressed, I looked through my cell to see what was going on in the city that day. A play in the park sounded fun to me, and I found one that I thought Ashton might enjoy too.

I was sitting in the living room when he came in. He had a bag in his hand and came to kiss me. "Hey, you. You're looking beautiful this morning."

"Thanks. You look rather dashing yourself." I got up to follow him into the kitchen. "And where did you get off to this morning?"

He placed the sack on the countertop, then proceeded to pull out everything inside of it. "I'm making up a new Sunday tradition. I cook breakfast, and you clean up the mess I make."

"Oh, yes!" I said with mock enthusiasm as I clapped my hands.

He stopped what he was doing to look at me with a questioning gaze. "I thought you said that you liked to clean when we were out at Artimus and Julia's house?"

"I did." I felt a little stupid for acting like a bitch. "Okay, we can make this a thing. So, what are you making?"

"I bought fresh blueberries. I'm going to try my hand at making homemade muffins. I like to bake, but I rarely do it because it makes a real mess and there are lots of bowls to wash." He patted me on the back. "But with you doing the cleaning, I think it might be fun. And Sunday is our fun day."

Putting an apron on myself, I took another one out of the drawer I'd put them in when I first bought them, and tied one around his waist. They matched: mine was a Minnie Mouse one, and his was Mickey Mouse. I thought we looked adorable.

"There's a play in the park today at one. You want to catch it?" I asked him as I looked over his shoulder at the recipe. "You want me to get out the bowls for you? I bought a set last week and put them away." I snapped my fingers. "And I got a set of measuring spoons too. I'll get them for you."

I had bought a number of things for his place. I couldn't help myself. It just seemed that every time I went shopping, I found this thing or that thing that would be perfect for him.

"What kind of play is it?" he asked me, then walked to the fridge to get out some eggs and milk.

"A love story." I placed the bowls on the counter for him. "Would you like to use the mixer I bought the other day? Or would a whisk be better?"

He smiled as he put the milk and eggs on the counter. "You sure have been buying a lot of stuff, Nina. The bathroom is nearly unrecognizable."

It hit me that he might not like me buying things for his home. "I'm sorry. I can take them back, I guess. I just thought they made the place homier is all."

With a laugh, he hugged me. "No, I like them all. I was just saying." He let me go and went to get the rest of the ingredients. "And the play sounds nice. I think a day in the park would be great."

As the morning went on, I noticed that he hadn't said one word about me staying Monday night too. Which was odd. And I felt kind of sad that he hadn't.

Maybe he's getting tired of me.

The muffins turned out perfect, and he made a care package for me to take to coffee with Lila and Julia the next day. "The girls will like them," he said as he boxed them up.

"You're quite the homemaker," I joked with him.

He pulled me into his arms and kissed me before saying, "So are you."

The play was nice, the weather good, and the day was going well. The only thing missing were his pleas for me to stay another night. And I was actually beginning to get upset by that.

Does he not really want me around?

It hadn't been easy to turn him down all those times. I had done it because his therapist didn't think the time was right for us to move in together.

As hard as it was to keep following her advice when all I wanted to do was be with him as much as I possibly could, I'd done what she wanted. And now it seemed that Ashton was getting used to me telling him no, so he wasn't going to ask anymore.

And that made me upset.

Never had I imagined that following her advice would lead to Ashton and I growing apart, but that's what it felt like. That wasn't the plan at all.

The plan was for us to grow closer and eventually become even more than just boyfriend and girlfriend. But now I was beginning to wonder.

After the play, we walked in the park, strolling around while holding hands and just enjoying the nice day. "Where would you like to eat dinner tonight?"

I thought about it for a second before answering. "Let's not eat out. Let's make spaghetti."

"Good idea. I'm with ya on that. We can get some good wine too." He began heading out of the park. "We can get some fresh spices for the meatballs."

Happy that we were going to cook together, I still couldn't say I was *entirely* happy. There was still no mention of staying another night.

We shopped then went back to his place and he took off to take a shower. "I got a little sweaty while we were out. I'm going to shower up real quick. Have a glass of wine, and we can start cooking when I get out."

Getting myself a glass of the red we'd bought, I took a seat on the sofa and put my feet up. The day had felt long to me. I couldn't say why. The only thing that really came to mind was the fact that I'd been waiting for him to say something that never came.

But even with all he hadn't said, he and I got along great, and he was every bit as attentive as he'd always been. There wasn't any need for me to be feeling upset.

I began to think I was being bratty about the whole thing. He'd been told 'no' as many times as he could handle, was my guess. I needed to get the hell over it.

But that proved harder to do than I'd thought. He came back out, smelling crisp and clean and looking fresh and handsome as ever. All I could think about was how nice it would be to come home with him after a long day of work. We could take a shower together, then get into bed.

But he won't ask me to stay anymore!

I was cutting up an onion when the words popped out of my mouth, "If you want me to stay tomorrow, I can."

"Oh?" He looked at me with confusion riddling his face. "I thought you said that was a bad idea."

"Yes, I have said that." I didn't know how to say the right words. I didn't want to come off as needy. "But you've asked me for weeks now. I feel like I was wrong, saying no so many times now."

"That's nice of you." He went on, forming a meatball. But he didn't say another word about me staying another night.

I waited awhile, chopping up some bell pepper too before I brought it up again. "So, do you want me to stay tomorrow night too?"

"I don't want you to do anything you feel isn't right, Nina." He put the finished meatballs into the oven to bake.

I didn't know what to say to that. So I finished what I was doing, and when we were all done, we ate in silence.

I felt awkward for even bringing the subject up. And now I was thoroughly confused about what he wanted.

Does he want me to stay or not?

At the end of the meal, he sat back and patted his stomach. "Another fine meal we've made, Nina. I think we make a great team. Don't you?"

"I do." I did think we made a good team, but I was still a little miffed that he'd given such a vague answer earlier and that the subject now seemed to be closed. I got up and took the dishes to the sink to rinse them before putting them in the dishwasher.

He came in behind me. "I've been wondering something. You may find this much too soon to ask, but what kind of wedding have you envisioned yourself having?"

Turning around to face him, I felt a bit shocked. He hadn't asked me to stay another night, even though I'd told him that I would, yet here he was asking me about what kind of wedding I wanted?

"Nothing special," I said, then got back to work.

"I see." He put the wine glasses next to the sink. Leaning over my shoulder, he said, "So, like a justice of the peace or something like that?"

"I suppose so." His close proximity went a long way toward soothing my annoyance. "I don't want anything big. I don't want to spend lots of money. I just want it to be small, quaint, and intimate."

"That's cool." He leaned back against the counter and crossed his arms. "I like that idea too."

"Good." I finished putting the dishes in the dishwasher, then closed it and started it up. The whirring sound was loud, so he took my hand to lead me out of the noisy kitchen.

He gently pushed me to take a seat on the sofa then handed me a little black box. I wasn't sure what he was doing. "Are you ...?"

Before I could finish, he said, "Don't ask. Just open the box."

When I pulled the top off, I saw a key. "And this is?"

"A key to the apartment. I want you to move in. I don't want you to stay four nights a week—I want you to stay all of them." He sat down beside me. "And before you say anything, I want you to know that Dr. Patel has given us her approval on this."

My mind went blank as I held the key in my hand. "We're moving in together?"

He nodded. "We are."

Throwing my arms around him, I began to cry. I was so happy.

Things were beginning to move forward!

CHAPTER TWENTY-SIX

Ashton

A busy workweek meant that moving Nina into our place was harder than anticipated. We had to wait for the weekend to get the majority of her things over. Luckily, she only had material possessions to move. She'd left all of her furniture there, selling it to the new tenant her roomie Sandy had found to take over her room.

Placing the last item of clothing in the closet, Nina turned to look at me with a smile plastered on her beautiful face. "That's it. I'm officially all moved in!"

I held out my arms, and she ran to jump into them. The kiss we shared felt ten times stronger than any one of our kisses before. Taking this step to make our union a bit more official seemed to be a stimulant for passion.

Light had yet to leave the sky, but our night was already beginning. Pushing the strap of her sundress off her shoulder, I moved my mouth to kiss a trail over her soft skin.

One hand moved through my hair as she made a quiet, purring sound. I moved my hand to push the other strap off, and soon her dress was puddled around her feet on the floor.

Picking her up, I carried her to the bed as I gazed into the golden depths of her gorgeous eyes. "I love you so much, Nina Kramer."

Her soft fingers moved over my cheek. "And I love you more than I knew was even possible, Ashton Lange."

The pink bra and panty set were all that separated her body from my prying and eager eyes. I stripped them away to look at her naked body as it lay on what was now 'our' bed.

The way my heart swelled in my chest told me that we had made the right choice. One day, in the not so distant future, this woman would take my name, and I knew that without a single doubt.

Starting at the tips of her toes, I kissed every last inch of her body before I came back to her lips. The smile she wore invigorated me. I brushed her dark blonde hair back, then kissed her cheeks, her forehead, the tip of her nose, and lastly, her sweet lips.

Breathing her in, I made myself let go of everything else but her. Nina had crept in, taking up every last part of me. She'd melded with my soul, bonded with my brain, and filled the empty spaces that had been left inside of me.

If there were such things as soulmates, Nina was mine.

She stared into my eyes once I'd released her lips. Moving her hands underneath my T-shirt, she lifted it over my head. Her hands went to work on the button and zipper of my shorts and she pushed them down. She hooked her fingers into the waistband of my boxer briefs, and then rid me of those too.

Moving me onto my back, she took her turn kissing me all over. But she started at the top and went south from there. Her lips caressed my skin, making no playful nips as she ran them all over my body.

My skin prickled with the electric sensation she left in her wake. I couldn't take my eyes off her as she moved her mouth over me. She kissed all the way to my toes, then moved back up. Her eyes were on my erect cock, but I wanted something else. I wanted to be inside of her.

Reaching out, I took her underneath her arms and picked her up as I sat up. Lifting her up, I let her back down on me, her tight pussy sliding down my cock. She put her feet out behind me and there we sat, like puzzle pieces, locked together.

I didn't need her to move just yet. I wanted to just sit there like that. We looked into each other's eyes, as close as we could be with me inside her, falling into each other in a way I had never done with anyone else.

We didn't need to say a word as we connected. A tear fell down her cheek, and I leaned in to kiss it away. I didn't need to ask why she was crying—I knew. Things were getting very real between us. We were both wide open and letting the other in. It was a beautiful thing.

My lips on her cheek moved down to take her mouth. The kiss was soft and loving. Our tongues moved gently with the others. Her tits squished against my chest and I felt her heart beating nice and slowly.

This was making love. We'd thought before that we'd made love, but we hadn't. This was sharing our love in its truest form. One day in the far away future we would be old and gray, unable to make the movements we were capable of at this time. In those days, I could see us holding each other this same way, relishing in the connection and needing nothing more than that to keep our love alive and well all through the years.

And with that one thought, my cock twitched. Nina's heartbeats increased, her body heated in my arms. With that one little movement, I'd spurred her on, changing the moment from one of pure love to pure lust.

She moved her body to grind on mine as our kiss went deeper, sexier, and hungrier.

My hands went hard on her body, gripping her back, pulling her closer to me. Her hands moved up to run through my hair. She pulled the band off the bun at the back of my head, releasing my hair so she could run her fingers all through it.

Lifting her up and down to stroke my cock, I held her by the waist as our kiss came to an end. Already panting, she moved her hands to my chest, pushing me to lie back. She moved her legs so that she was straddling me. Riding me hard, I watched her boobs as they jiggled with every move she made.

I had to take them into my hands to squeeze them, they were so tempting. I sat up and sucked one of them as I played with the other. She moaned as her nails dug into the flesh of my back, "Ashton ... Baby ... Yes!"

The next time I opened my eyes, the bedroom had gone dark. I rolled over with her, mounting her as I pulled her legs up, putting her feet by her head. Pushing my cock into her much deeper, I loved the deep grunt that came from her as I shoved my meaty organ into her tight recesses.

Each thrust I gave had her making the same little grunt. No matter how much I gave her, she would take. She hung onto my wrists as I slammed into her over and over until I felt liquid heat pour from her as her body climaxed.

Her pussy pulsed around my cock incessantly, trying to pull me under with her. I let her legs go, bringing them down. She wrapped them around me as she arched up to me. "Harder," came her one demand.

My cock was ready to burst as I thrust into her fast and hard. Her pussy pulsed around me as she clung to me, screaming my name over and over until I could take no more.

I let it all go, filling her with my seed then going limp and falling onto her body, our skin slick with sweat. I could feel her heart as it pounded inside her chest.

I hadn't known such an exchange was possible. We both left it all on the table that night. Not an ounce of shame or shyness was left in either of us. I felt like she was just as much a part of me as I was. And I was the same for her.

Moving to one side, I trailed my fingers over her stomach. I didn't say a word, but thought to myself that one day I would see that belly nice and round, filled with my child.

My future resided inside of her. Nina Kramer was and always had been my future. The one woman for me.

And just as I thought that, my eyes began to burn. They filled with tears. Natalia filled my mind. The image burned my brain. The memory of her came on so suddenly and with an intensity that I couldn't have foreseen.

I had thought she was my one and only, too. It had been her.

What's happening to me?

A hand moved over my chest, then Nina's sweet face was close enough for me to see. Her lips pressed against my forehead. "It's going to be okay, Ashton. There's room for both of us in your heart. You don't have to worry." She kissed away every last tear before she said, "The love you have for each of us is different. But you can't have a love like ours with a person who is no longer here. She understands that, I assure you. Your love for her isn't gone. It's just resting in the back of your mind. You'll never completely lose her. Don't worry."

Gripping her hand, I choked out a sob. "What did I do to deserve you?"

"Hush, now." She kissed my cheek. "You and I were meant to be. Life is a crazy thing. A rollercoaster ride. And with any ride comes danger. Some make it to the end, and some don't. That's just the way that it is. It doesn't mean that one is more important than another. It's just the way life goes."

Finally, I regained my composure. "If she'd lived, I would've never had this with you. I would've never known how great things could be."

"That's right." Nina's lips pressed against mine. "And I wouldn't have ever known this either. I'm sorry you were a part of the accident that took Natalia's life. I'm sorry you bear guilt over that. But I think you should know that nothing happens for no reason at all. Nothing, Ashton."

I lay there, thinking about what I had just experienced. It was life-changing. It didn't make much sense to me that a sexual act could be felt that deeply, like soul-shatteringly deep. But it was real. It was intense. And it was definitely meant to be.

Slipping my arm around Nina's shoulders, I pulled her close, kissing the top of her head. "There's no doubt in my mind that we were meant to be together, Nina. Whether it happened this way or another, it couldn't have been a mistake."

"I think the same thing." She snuggled into my side. "I wonder if we'll have an even more intense experience after we get married." She laughed. "Listen to me. You haven't even asked me to marry you and here I am, talking like you have. Ignore me. I'm just riding the high of our delightful bed-play."

"One day, Nina Kramer." I kissed the side of her head. "One day, you'll be Nina Lange, and we will have our happily ever after. You just wait and see."

A long sigh came out of her. "I can wait. I can do anything for you, Ashton. Anything at all."

As I lay there, holding her close, I could swear again that the woman could read my mind. There just wasn't any other explanation for how she always knew exactly what I needed to hear.

So, I thought one last thought before I fell asleep.

I will love you forever, Nina Kramer.

CHAPTER TWENTY-SEVEN

Nina

The next few months flew by. Living with Ashton was better than a dream come true. We had more fun than I thought two humans could possibly have. Even chores were fun when we did them together.

Taking the laundry down to the laundry room in the basement of the building, we told each other scary stories to make the time pass by more quickly.

I came up with a great one. "So, I ran into an old woman the other day in the elevator. She told me she's lived here for seventy years."

"That long?" he asked with surprise. "I've never seen anyone that old in this building. Are you sure?"

Nodding, I went on with my little story. "I'm sure. She said she lives on the top floor. She rarely gets out. Has her groceries delivered." I decided to add that to make the tale more plausible.

"Okay," he said, but looked skeptical. "So, what else did you and this old woman talk about?"

I ran my hands up and down my arms, as if I'd gotten chills. Which I hadn't, but I was going to milk this story for all it was worth.

"She asked me if I'd been down to the basement, to which I answered that I had. It's where the laundry room is located, after all."

"Uh huh," he said, as he put more quarters in the dryer. "A laundry room that could use some new machines, if you ask me. This is the third time I'm having to start this dryer."

"Take it up with the manager, Ashton." I rolled my eyes before going on with the story. "Okay, so what this lady told me was that there was a man who lived here even before she did. And that man was the janitor for this building. One day, he was caught taking some kids and hiding them away in this very dungeon. Oops. I mean, basement."

Now Ashton rolled his eyes. "Oh, yeah? And what did he do to these supposed kids, Nina?"

I weighed the options before saying, "He ate them!"

With a grimace, he said, "Gross." Then he went to pull the clothes out of one of the washers. "These are ready to go into a dryer now."

I took the buggy over and let him fill it with the wet clothes before taking them to put them into an empty dryer. "The parents of the kids found him in this very basement one day, and they killed him."

"And how did they do that?" he asked me, with a grin on his face.

Looking around, I found the old furnace and pointed at it. "They threw him in that thing. And the really creepy part is that ..."

He chimed in, "He comes to people who live in this building in their sleep and tries to kill them."

Shrugging, I said, "Sounds like you have heard this story, Ashton."

"Yeah, it's called *Nightmare on Elm Street*." He laughed uproariously as he slapped his thighs. "You'll have to come up with something original if you want to get one past me, doll. I've watched every horror flick ever made."

"I hadn't even realized I was making up a story that already existed. I suppose I saw it sometime when I was a kid or something." I laughed. "Funny, huh?"

"I guess so." He put four quarters into the dryer. "I hope this one works better than that other one. I don't want to spend our entire Sunday down here."

"What are your plans for today?" I asked him, as we hadn't discussed anything fun to do yet.

"I've got plans, baby. Big plans. And they don't involve going anywhere at all," he informed me.

I was a little displeased with his announcement though. "Aw. Why not?"

He pinched my cheek as she smiled at me. "No reason to whine, baby. You'll like it. I promise."

"Can you give me a hint about what we'll be doing?" I asked, as I pushed the buggy back to the corner it was kept in.

"Well, I'll be making you a great lunch. And we'll be enjoying it picnic style, on the living room floor." He made a flourishing gesture, as if he was throwing a blanket on the floor.

"Why not just have a real picnic outside? In a park, maybe. Now that sounds fun too, doesn't it?" I asked, trying to get him to do something outside of the house.

He nodded. "That sounds fun too, but this has to be done just the way I've already planned."

I could see I wasn't going to get him to change his mind, so I stopped trying. We finished the laundry with him telling me a story that actually did freak me out, making it hard to walk up the stairs to leave the basement. "Now I keep thinking a hand is going to come out from under one of these stairs and grab my ankle, Ashton. Thanks a lot!"

"That's what I'm here for, to make life interesting for you, baby." He laughed at his joke as I walked carefully, so as not to fall when something did grab me.

Fortunately, I made it up the stairs, and we went up to our apartment. I put the laundry away as he set about getting this special lunch prepared. He laid out a blanket for us that spread out over the living room floor.

He'd pushed the furniture back to make room for the feast he'd made. I could smell the smoked ham as I put things away in the bedroom. "That smells awesome, babe," I called out to him.

"I'm putting everything on the blanket now. Are you nearly done in there?" he asked me.

Putting away the towels, I shouted back, "Yep. Are you ready for me?"

"I am," he called out.

Taking a second to look in the bathroom mirror, I ran my hand through my hair, then over my T-shirt to smooth out a few wrinkles. "Not too shabby."

Heading to the living room, I found Ashton lying on his side, his upper body resting on his arm as he looked at me. "Hey, you." He patted the blanket. "Come take a seat."

I sat down with my legs crossed in front of him. "Okay. So, what do we have here?"

Stretching his hand out, he gestured to the food. "We have smoked ham, potato salad, and green beans. And some white wine to go with that." He sat up, getting on both of his knees as he dug into the pocket of his shorts. "But first, I've got something to ask you."

I thought he must have tickets to something in that pocket and had planned on surprising me with a show of some kind for our fun day. I clapped. "Oh, goody!"

He moved around a bit, getting on one knee as he held out a little white box. Flipping the lid open, he grinned as my eyes focused on the gorgeous diamond ring inside.

My hands flew to my mouth. "Nina Velma Kramer, would you do me the great honor of becoming my lawfully wedded wife?"

Tears clouded my vision as I nodded, but there was a massive knot in my throat that prevented me from saying a single word. But my nod was enough for him, and he took my left hand, sliding the ring onto my finger.

Wiping my eyes with the back of my free hand, I finally choked out, "Yes."

"Good to hear you say the word, Nina." Ashton laughed, then crawled over to me. His lips touched mine, and I threw my arms around him.

"I can't believe you did this today, Ashton!" I was crying like a baby. "This is the best day of my life!"

"I hope to be responsible for many more of your best days, baby. Many, many more." He got up, picking me up with him and we danced around the room to no music at all.

I was soaring as we swayed, and I looked at the ring he'd given me. "It's so beautiful. I'll never take it off. I swear I won't."

He laughed again, and then we kissed. For the longest time ever, we kissed and held each other like we never had before. He'd made the perfect Sunday fun day. I would never forget it.

After settling down, we ate the lunch he'd made, and I had to run one little errand. "I've got to get down to the corner store. I've been feeling little cramps, so I'm thinking I'd better get some tampons in this place before Mother Nature hits me."

"I'll go with you," he said, as he hauled the dishes to the kitchen.

"You don't have to." I waved him off. "It'll only take me a few minutes and then I'll be right back. I think I'd like to meet you in the bed when I get back. Naked and waiting, as a good fiancé should."

Jerking his head at the blanket picnic that still had to be cleaned up, he said, "After I get this taken care of, I will dutifully undress and wait for my fiancée, as requested."

"Cool. I'll be right back." I grabbed my wallet and house key, then left to go to the market.

The sidewalk was crowded as usual when I stepped outside. The air was on the brisk side, and that always made people walk a bit faster. I stepped in with everyone, making my way to the market at the end of the block.

Some man was yelling at someone over his cell as he walked past me. At first I jumped, thinking he was yelling at me. "Hey, you listen to me, bitch."

Whoever he was talking to was an idiot, as far as I was concerned. Anyone who would call me a name like that would've been hung up on before he could say one more word.

The jackass's voice faded as he moved ahead of me. Somewhere in the distance, I could hear the sound of a car honking continuously. It wouldn't let up, and it was coming closer.

Moving a bit closer to the inside of the sidewalk, I was getting ready to go into the door of the market. Some idiot boys cut in, cutting me off and stopping me dead in my tracks as they played some game of chase or something. "Hey, you little shits!"

One of them actually pushed me into the way of another boy, shouting, "You'll never catch me, Joey!"

Joey pushed me out of his way, as if I wasn't even a real person. "Ha, fuck you, Ray-Ray! I'll get you. You'll see."

As they ran off into the pack of people, I turned around to get back to the entrance of the market. Now I was muttering obscenities under my breath, "Damn little bastards. Where are their parents? Heathens!"

Some man shouted, "Move!"

I stopped to look back to see who was being rude now. I had just about had it with rude people. I was ready to chew his ass out, no matter who he was or how big he was. "Now, see here," I shouted.

But the crowd was parting, people running in every direction. The sound of the horn was so loud that I couldn't think.

"Move!" came the loud order again. Only this time it was a woman who had said it. "Get the hell out of the way!"

I didn't know which way to turn. People were going every which way. Horror filled me as three people who had been in front of me seconds ago, suddenly weren't.

"He's driving through everyone!" came another shout.

And then the grill of a truck was right there in front of me. Barreling toward me, mowing down everyone in its path.

Including me.

CHAPTER TWENTY–EIGHT

Ashton

With the picnic cleaned up, I walked toward the bedroom to get undressed and ready for my new fiancée. I laughed as I thought about the expression on her face when she first saw the ring.

Getting into the bedroom, I thought I would open up a window to let in a little fresh air. And as I did, I could hear the sounds of sirens filtering through from the street below.

Looking down, I could see that things didn't look right. People were moving oddly. Running or stumbling in every direction. And then my eyes went to something that just shouldn't have been there. An armored truck was up on the sidewalk.

My heart stopped as I saw police cars stopped on every side of the vehicle. Officers got out with guns drawn, aiming them at the vehicle. Then a loud voice came up to me as one of the officers used a bullhorn, "Get out of the car with your hands up."

Pulling my cell out of my pocket, I found my hands were shaking as I swiped Nina's name. The phone rang, and I could hear it in the apartment. She'd left her phone on the nightstand. "Fuck!"

Hauling ass, I ran to get to the elevator. I had to get to Nina. I couldn't sit there and wait.

But I wasn't the only one rushing out to check on someone they cared about on the outside of that building. It took no time at all for the elevator to be filled with people, all trying to get to the ground floor.

The doorway became jammed as everyone tried to get out at the same time. "Everyone, just calm down," some man called out. "One at a time, people."

Panic had set in, and everyone was out for their own self. Finally, I made it out and moved in the direction I knew Nina had gone. Then everyone froze when the sound of a gunshot rang out.

I climbed up on a pole to see what I could. The police were moving fast toward the armored truck. Then I saw an officer waving, and more came in. An ambulance pulled up, and the officers took the person, who had obviously shot himself, to the back of it.

It was only then that I saw the people lying on the sidewalk. I couldn't make any one of them out. I looked around at the people around me in the crowd, searching desperately for Nina's face.

When I didn't find it, I got off the pole and tried my best to get to that truck. Praying the whole time that she was safe inside the store, I pushed my way through the mass of people.

When I got close to where I wanted to go, a strong arm stopped me. "No one can go any further than this." An office had stopped me.

"My wife is down here. I need to find her," I implored him.

"There are lots of wives and husbands down here, mister. You'll have to wait, just like everyone else." He gave me a slight push to get back, and it only made me mad.

"Listen to me," I said through gritted teeth.

The sound of more ambulances made me look up. Three stopped, and the paramedics got out. They swarmed through the people who were standing around. "Clear this entire area," one of them said. "We've got to be able to see to the wounded."

My heart stopped when someone called out, "We've got an unresponsive civilian over here."

Another called out, "No pulse here."

"Get them on the trucks," someone else shouted.

I watched as people were placed on stretchers, strapped down then taken to the backs of the waiting ambulances. Those three drove away, and three more came in right behind them.

The same thing followed. The paramedics searched, found, and took away. But this time I saw dark blonde hair falling across the top of the stretcher. "Hey, wait!"

The cop turned to give me a frown. "I thought I told you ..."

"I think that's her." I pointed at the moving stretcher that was about to be put into the ambulance. "Please just let me see if it's her."

He moved his arm then jerked his head. "Hurry up."

I ran toward the stretcher and every step I took made my blood drop a degree colder. When I got all the way to them, I finally saw her face. Blood ran in tiny rivers from her forehead and nose. "Oh, God!" I felt my knees buckle.

"Do you know her?" one of the paramedics asked.

"She's my wife." I knew that they wouldn't let me see her if I told them anything else—I had learned that the hard way once before.

"Come on," the man said as he and the other paramedic put her inside the ambulance.

I climbed in to sit on the other side of her as one of them went to work putting in an IV, and the other closed the doors and rushed to the driver's seat to take us to a hospital.

"Is she ..." I couldn't make myself say the word.

The paramedic knew what I wanted to hear. "Her heart is beating, and she is breathing on her own. So, yes, she's alive. For now, anyway." He moved his hand in a circle over her stomach. That's when I noticed that blood was seeping onto the blanket that covered her. "She's going to need to go straight into surgery. She has wounds on her stomach, and from the bloating, I would guess internal hemorrhaging as well."

"That truck hit her?" I asked.

He nodded. "She seems to be the last person he hit before he stopped. She made it out better than some. A few are still trapped under the vehicle and won't be helped until they can get it moved. With the crowd, it slows everything down."

"Fucking New York," I muttered. "I'm getting her the hell out of here."

The way he looked down had me worried. I stared at him until he looked at me. "I hope you get that chance." He looked at the ring I had just put on her finger. "Look, she'll be going straight into surgery. You should take her ring, so it doesn't get lost or something. What's her name, by the way?"

He pulled the engagement ring off her finger and dropped it into my palm. "It's Nina Kramer."

He wrote that down on the paper he had on a clipboard. "You should call her family. They should be here."

I knew it was serious, but I had no idea it was that serious. "I will. I'll call them." I took her hand as it fell out from under the blanket. "Nina, you have to pull through this for me. You know you've got to do it, baby. You can't leave me here. Please don't leave me here. I can't be alone again. I can't." I broke down then. I couldn't hold it in. I begged her and begged her to stay with me.

When we got to the hospital, I walked as far as they would let me, holding her hand and telling her not to leave me, all the way down the long hall.

When we got to the double doors, where family could no longer go, I fell to my knees. Turning my head up to God, I prayed for him to please not take her yet. *Please, let her stay with me.*

Someone put his hands on my shoulders. "Come on. Let's get you to a waiting room."

Some big man wearing white scrubs picked up me and let me lean on him as he took me to a quiet, empty room. He helped me sit down, then handed me a box of tissues. "Thank you." I pulled one out and blew my nose.

"Hey, I've been there." He patted me on the shoulder.

"This is my second time being here." I wiped my eyes, but I had no idea why I'd done that. It wasn't like the tears had stopped flowing.

"Second time?" he asked with concern. "Man, that's rough. All you can do is pray now, mister. Pray hard, and don't stop until she's better. You hear me?"

I nodded. "Pray until she's better. I hear you." The only thing he didn't know was that I had done that before too. It hadn't worked then. Why should it work now?

When my cell rang, I didn't even jump, that's how numb I was. I saw it was Artimus. "She's hurt," I answered his call, cutting off his immediate question about the attack and whether we'd been home when it happened.

"Shit," came his quick reply. "We'll come to you, Ashton. I'll get Julia to call her family."

"Thank you." I gasped to catch my breath. "I'm losing it. I really am. I've never felt so helpless and lost. Not ever. This is worse than last time. I can't do it alone. I can't."

"You don't have to. We're on our way. Just hang tight. We've got you, buddy." He ended the call, and I fell back in the chair.

My life was falling apart once again. I had no idea what I was supposed to do. How I could possibly go on if she left me.

I put her ring on my pinky finger. It only fit partially. Holding it to my lips, I kissed it as I prayed, "Please don't take her too, God. I'll do anything if you just don't take her away from me."

It felt as if an eternity had passed before anyone I knew showed up. Duke and Lila rushed to me. Lila got to me first, hugging me tightly. "She's going to be okay, Ashton. Don't worry."

I pushed her back, hoping like hell she'd been able to talk to someone who had told her that. "Did you get to talk to someone about how she's doing in surgery?"

Her blue eyes went blank. "She's in surgery?"

"You didn't know?" I asked in surprise.

She shook her head then Duke got to us. "What the hell happened, Ashton?"

"There was some kind of attack. This armored truck hit her. She's got internal injuries, they said, and her head was bleeding too." I gulped as I sat back down. "They took her straight into surgery as soon as she got here."

"Was she talking?" Lila asked.

"No." I shook my head. "She was knocked out."

"By the drugs they gave her to help with the pain?" Duke asked hopefully.

"No." I tried to put logical words together but found it was hard to do. "Unconscious. That's how they found her."

Lila put her hand on mine as she sat on one side of me and Duke sat on the other. "Was she breathing?"

I nodded. "Yeah." My hands moved over my face. "Blood was running like this over her face. Her nose was bleeding." My hand went to my stomach. "There was blood on the blanket around her stomach."

The color ran out of Lila's face. "I see."

Duke ran his arm behind me to put it on Lila's shoulder. "We've got to have faith here, you guys. We can't lose hope now. She's a fighter. She was breathing when she came in. That's better than nothing."

It was barely better than nothing. But he was right. It was something. Natalia hadn't fared so well after the accident. Nina wasn't as bad off as she'd been.

I closed my eyes and begged God to give Nina a chance. I knew I couldn't go on without her. I had no idea what would happen to me if she didn't make it.

I looked at Duke. He was a great friend to me. And the only one I knew who could stand up to Artimus. Artimus wouldn't let me go, but Duke might. "Duke, if she dies, just let me go, okay?"

CHAPTER TWENTY-NINE

Nina

"He's not going to make it," I heard a woman whispering.

My eyes fluttered open as I heard a very slow, beeping sound. Only a dim light filled the small room I was in. One wall was entirely made out of glass, and I could see a woman in pale pink scrubs standing across the hallway.

She looked on as a couple of other people, also wearing scrubs, stood inside the other room. That's where the slow, beeping sound was coming from.

The door to the room I was in stood wide open, and it was made of glass too. I moved my arm. Or I tried to, anyway. I stopped trying to move it when I felt something tugging at it.

My head turned slowly, and I found I was hooked up to some clear lines. It seemed I was in the hospital, and apparently in bad shape. But I couldn't recall just why that was.

When the beeping sound went from slow to one constant beep, I knew the person in the other room had died. My brain was in a fog, but even with the haze around it, I wondered if Ashton had been with me when I was hurt.

And then I wondered if that was him in the room across the hall-way. Wondered if it was him whose heart had stopped beating.

"Help," I croaked out. But no one heard me.

"Call the time," one of the women in scrubs said.

"Two-fifteen a.m. is the official time of death," another woman said from inside the room. I couldn't see her as she stood behind the curtain, which had been pulled across the majority of the glass wall.

I could see the foot of the hospital bed, though. In that bed, some person had just died, and I lay there, helpless to find out if it was Ashton or not.

Closing my eyes, I tried not to think that it was him. I couldn't take it if it was him. If I lost him, I had no idea what I would do. I had never loved anyone as much as I loved him, and I knew I would never love anyone else that way ever again.

I was sure my heart would give out too if it was Ashton who now lay lifeless in the bed across the hall.

"You can call the nursing home to let them know Mr. Sandstone won't be coming back," someone said with a hushed voice.

Mr. Sandstone?

My eyes flew back open.

It's not Ashton!

I was elated to hear the lady say a name that I didn't know at all. And then I felt terrible for being so happy when a person had just died. And one so close to me.

Well, I didn't actually know Mr. Sandstone. We weren't mentally close, but physically, we were only a few feet away from each other. I needed to show more reverence, I thought.

Hell, he was probably floating away, looking back at us all and thinking that I was a pretty heartless bitch to be looking so happy and smiling so big when he'd just passed away.

"Sorry, Mr. Sandstone. Rest in peace," I offered.

The nurses began to leave the room as some men came in to deal with the dead body. And one of them spotted me looking at them. "Hi there, Nina." She waved to get another person's attention. "Look whose woken up."

Three of the nurses came into my room. One went to check the machines, as the other two gave me wide smiles. I could see their last names were on the tags they had on their shirts.

The woman closest to me had *Gonzales* on her tag. "Nurse Gonzales, my throat hurts, it's so dry. Can I have something to drink?"

The other nurse ran off. "I'll get her some water."

"Everything's looking good here," the last nurse said.

Nurse Gonzales leaned over me, flashing a small light in my eyes. "Normal pupil dilation. Well, normal for being on morphine." She put her hand on my shoulder as she held up two fingers. "Can you tell me how many fingers I'm holding up?"

"Two," I answered. "Now, can anyone tell me what the heck has happened to me?"

Nurse Gonzales took the lead, as the other nurse excused herself to go check on the others. Whoever the others were. "Someone drove their car into a crowded sidewalk. You were hit by a pretty big truck."

"Damn." I was glad to see the other nurse coming back to my room with a little pink cup in her hand.

"Here you are," Nurse Sloan said as she handed me a drink with a small straw in it. "Now, take little sips. It's been awhile since you've had any liquid down your throat."

I sipped it and had to stop myself from chugging it down. My throat was bone-dry. "How long have I been here?" I asked, when I'd drunk my fill.

"Two weeks," came Nurse Gonzales' reply. "The incident happened two weeks ago. You were one of the first ones brought in."

I had been out for two weeks and hadn't even known it. The next thing on my mind had nothing to do with my injuries. "Has anyone been coming to see me?"

"Your family has," Nurse Sloan told me. "And your coworkers too." She smiled at me as she went to the bottom of the bed, picking up one of my feet and massaging it as she lifted it up. "They wanted to fill this room with flowers and balloons and such, but that's not allowed in ICU. You're allowed one visitor at a time and for only five minutes. And that's only once an hour, for a few hours in the morning and a couple in the evening. That's why no one is here with you. It's not because no one cares about you; it's just the policy at our hospital for patients in Intensive Care."

"So, I'm in bad shape then," I surmised from my situation. "But I don't feel any pain."

"You're on a morphine drip. That's why you're not feeling any pain," Nurse Gonzales filled me in. "But we're lowering the amount of that morphine hourly. We wanted you to wake up. And by later on today, around noon or so, the morphine will be taken away."

The other nurse looked at me with a little frown. "And then you will feel a bit of discomfort."

"Great." I thought about what I'd said and how I'd sounded. "That was whiny. I shouldn't be like that. I should be happy that I'm going to feel things again. I should be happy that I'm alive."

"Yes, you should." Nurse Gonzales took a seat in the large rocker next to my bed. "You had some pretty bad internal injuries and one to your brain, too. Thank goodness the one to your brain was minor. But your organs took a beating. Your liver had a laceration. Your kidneys were so badly bruised, they shut down for a few days. Your heart just kept on ticking though. You've got yourself an amazingly strong heart, honey."

And that heart was feeling a little down in the dumps as I looked at my left hand to find my engagement ring was gone. From what I could recall, I had just gotten proposed to. Ashton had slid a big diamond ring on my finger. Or had that just been a dream while I was under?

I had to ask them about him. "Has there been a man who has come to see me?"

"You've had a few come to see you," Nurse Gonzales said. "Lots of staff members from the network have been stopping by to say quick hellos to you."

"But no man in particular has come by to see me more than the rest?" I asked, losing hope fast.

Ashton might've taken off the ring himself. He might have been freaked out by my near-death experience. Hell, he may have flown the coop, for all I knew.

"Honey, the way you've been kept this last couple of weeks, no one has had much access to you," she told me. "Your momma is about the only one we all know by name. She's the main one who's been keeping up with your progress and passing that information on to everyone else who cares about you."

"Now that I'm awake, is there any chance that I'll get to have visitors for longer amounts of time?" I crossed my fingers, hoping she would say yes.

Her lips quirked up to one side. "Well, not a ton of time, but it will increase to fifteen minutes. The amount of visits per day will stay the same until you're put into a regular room."

"How long will I be here?" I looked up at the ceiling, feeling somewhat desperate.

"Well, there's just no telling, Nina." She looked at me with a vague smile. "You're getting better, but there are never any certainties with internal or brain injuries. I don't want to give you any number of days right now. But the doctor who's taking care of you will come in around seven this morning, and he might be able to give you some more answers."

I was already coming up with questions I needed to ask him. But the number one question on my mind was where Ashton was. I knew she didn't have an answer for that.

The nurse got up and handed me the remote to the television. "You can watch some TV, if you want to. That button there will call us if you want anything. Don't hesitate to push it if you there's anything you need."

I thought for a moment. "Should I call one of you guys if I have to use the bathroom?"

She laughed. "You're not getting out of that bed, sweetie. We've got you taken care of in that department. Just chill out. Sleep, watch the tube, and most of all, let your body heal while you rest. Think of this as the ultimate vacation. People are here to wait on you hand and foot. You won't have to lift a finger while you're in ICU. Not even to bathe yourself." She winked at me. "You're getting the five-star treatment, my lady."

Leaving me with a wave, I liked her already. "Hey, thanks for taking care of me, Nurse Gonzales."

"Thanks for being such a great patient." She gave me another wink. "But so far, you've been an unconscious one. Let's hope you're a great patient when you're awake too."

"I'll try to be." I watched her leave and felt a little weird.

I was all alone now. And in a hospital, of all places. I had no idea if I was still an engaged woman or not. I had no idea if I was even still in a relationship with Ashton. I had no idea about anything.

This much I knew for sure: Ashton would not be handling this well. Worst- case scenario, he'd see this as a sign. Maybe even think he was cursed or something.

One fiancée died in a crash, and one was nearly killed in an attack. *What are the freaking chances of that happening?*

Yeah, I could totally see Ashton thinking that he had some type of a curse going on.

He might have pulled the ring off my finger and retracted the proposal just because he thought that might save my life. And maybe it had.

I lay there thinking about Ashton, and as I did, I overheard one of the other nurses talking to someone, "Yeah, she died once on the operating table and once right there in that bed. We had to bring her back twice. She's a real miracle, that Nina Kramer."

Oh, shit!

Maybe Ashton is cursed!

CHAPTER THIRTY

Ashton

"Her mother called me this morning," I told Artimus as I sat in his office. "She's awake."

A frown furrowed his brow. "And you're sitting here because?"

I had the ring in my pocket, playing with it as I thought about why I was sitting in my boss's office instead of in the ICU waiting room. Waiting for my five-minute turn with Nina. "I do not know the answer to that."

"Is it because you're afraid?" he asked.

Shaking my head, I knew it wasn't fear that had me staying put after the call I'd gotten from her joy-filled mother that morning. "It's not that I'm afraid of anything. It's more like a veil of doubt."

He looked aggravated as he put his fingers on his forehead, massaging what must've been a headache. "Doubt about what?"

The crazy thing was that I had prayed so much for Nina to get better, and I'd thought I would blaze a trail to that hospital the minute I got word that she was awake and coherent. I would rush to her side and slip the engagement ring right back onto her long, slender finger. I would kiss her sweet lips and tell her everything was going to be all right. But I wasn't doing any of those things.

Pulling my hand out of my pocket with the ring on my pinky finger, I held it up. "Artimus, do you think there are such things as curses?"

"No," came his curt answer. "There are no curses. What's the deal with the ring, Ashton? What are you thinking?"

"I put a ring on Natalia's finger, and less than a year later, she was dead." I moved the ring, so the light made the diamond sparkle brightly. "Flash forward four years, and I put a ring on Nina's finger. Now, not even a day goes by before a fucking terrorist nearly kills her." I looked into Artimus' eyes. "A goddamned terrorist, Artimus. What are the odds? Please, tell me what they are. I need to know."

"First of all, in this day and age, being killed or hurt by a terrorist is not that uncommon." He got up and walked to the window to look out of it. "This isn't the only city that experiences such things. Even if you moved to some small town, it wouldn't be a guarantee that something like this wouldn't happen to you again."

"Then what am I supposed to do?" I had to know. "And how am I supposed to believe that Nina will be okay if I put this ring back on her finger?"

He turned to look at me, his face a puzzle of torment. "Ashton, you're letting your imagination take hold of you. If you keep thinking this way, you'll end up a lonely man. Is that what you want?"

"I don't want anyone to get hurt just because they love me." I put the ring on the desk and the overhead light refracted off it, making it glow. "That looks pretty powerful, sitting there, doesn't it? It's almost as if that ring has powers we can't understand."

He strode over, snapping the ring up as he growled, "Ashton Lange, you stop this right now. I won't let you do this to yourself again. Get your ass up, take this ring, and put it back on Nina's finger. Marry that woman and raise kids with her. Make her your family, Ashton. And put this idiotic idea out of your head. Accidents happen. That's that." He put the ring in my jacket pocket then took a seat. "And when is the last time that you talked to Dr. Patel, anyway?"

"Yesterday." I sighed, feeling the weight of the ring in my pocket. "Honestly, I wasn't feeling this way then. This just came up."

"Well, let it just go away the same way it popped up, then." He slammed his fist down on the desk. "You've got to stop thinking this way, and you've got to get over to that hospital and let the woman you love see your face. I'm sure she's missed you."

I shrugged. "She's been asleep. I'm sure she hasn't missed me. Maybe she's even had enough time to get over me—who wants to be the fiancée of a man whose fiancées keep dying? Maybe that's for the best."

"Get your ass up and get to that hospital." He stood up and went toward the door. "Once you see her. Once you talk to her, you'll stop this shit." He opened the door and pointed my way out. "Go!"

I got up slowly. I wasn't as gung-ho as he wanted me to be, but I would go see her. For the five minutes they would allow me to. But I wasn't sure if I would saddle her with the ring yet. I wasn't sure it would be safe to put it on her just yet. Maybe never.

Leaving the office with Artimus glaring at me, I got on the elevator. Moving the ring from the pocket of my jacket, I put it back in my pants pocket and let my fingers move around it.

My head wasn't right as I took a cab over to the hospital. Thoughts came and went as I stared at the floor.

Am I really cursed?

Should I leave Nina alone for her own good?

Should I just be alone for the rest of my life?

Would that be safer for everyone?

Will I ever be able to get over Nina?

I sighed heavily as I thought about that. I had hardly slept at all since the attack. And even as I thought about that and knew that the lack of sleep could contribute to depression, I ignored that fact.

Nina had made the apartment hers already, and I felt her presence there every day, even as she lay in the hospital unconscious and on the brink of death. Her things were everywhere. I tried to snuggle with her pillow to get some sleep, but that only put me to sleep for short spurts of time.

I needed her now. But was it my need for her that had gotten her hurt?

"Do you believe in curses?" I asked the cab driver.

"Oh! Yes, I do. Very much so," he told me as he bobbed his head.

"I think I'm cursed." I pulled the engagement ring out and held it up. "I think that when I put an engagement ring on a woman's finger that it puts them in great danger."

The driver stopped at a light and cocked his head to one side. "Let me get this straight. You have put that same ring on multiple women's fingers, and they've been hurt?"

Looking at the ring, I shook my head. "No, not this same ring. The rings are different."

"Oh, then, no," he informed me. "That's not a curse, then. If it were the same ring, then I would say it was a curse. Not the same ring —no curse."

I frowned, feeling a little dazed by the conversation and how quickly he'd shot down my theory about being cursed. "Maybe I'm just afraid of losing another partner, then, and that's what has me looking for explanations in the form of curses."

"Most likely, sir." His dark eyes looked at me through the rearview mirror. "I suppose then that you have lost a love, and now you have a new one and you think you might lose her too?"

Nodding, I confirmed his suspicions, "Yep."

"My advice is to push that worry away. If we let the worry of what might happen stop us, we will never do a damn thing. Or love anyone, for that matter. There is always a chance that something can happen to anyone. Or the chance that they will fall out of love with us and leave us one day. But we do it anyway." He winked at me. "Do you know why we do it anyway, sir?"

"I really don't." I shook my head, thinking that he hadn't helped me at all.

"We do it anyway because life encourages us to." His head bobbed again as he smiled. "Life is what it's all about, sir."

My eyes went back to the floor, not feeling like I was quite getting what he was saying. And there I spotted something that I hadn't noticed before when I'd been staring at the floor. A small piece of white paper. Like the fortune from a fortune cookie.

Picking it up, I read it: *In the end, it's not the years in your life that count, it's the life in your years.*

Holding the ring in one hand and the little paper with the wise words on it in the other, I thought about those words meant. I could have a life, long and free of worry, sadness, and loss. But what I would be giving up companionship, connection, and the highest price of all would be love.

I would have to give up love. And I would have to take my love away from Nina.

I had never thought about it that way.

I had lived four years without love in my life. Those years seemed so empty to me now. Did I want more empty years ahead of me? Or did I want years, no matter how few or how many there would be, that were full of life? A life that included love, happiness, and Nina?

The cab driver stopped in front of the entrance to the hospital, and I put the engagement ring on my pinky finger. "You know what?"

"What, sir?" he asked me as he turned to look back at me.

"I choose life. Have a very nice day." I got out of the cab, listening to the man laugh.

He made a joyful sound as he laughed and called out to me from the open window, "You have a nice life, sir."

"I think I will." I went inside, greeting everyone I saw. "Good morning. Nice day, isn't it?" I went all the way to the waiting room in ICU where I found a nurse with a nametag that said *Gonzales*. "Hi there. Good morning, Nurse Gonzales. I know I'm five minutes late for this morning's visiting hours, but I've got to see my girl. You've got her back there, and I need to put this little ring back on her finger." I wiggled my pinky to let her see the ring.

"Ah." She smiled. "You must be here to see Nina Kramer. She's been asking her mother about you. I had no idea you two were engaged. You never mentioned it."

"I wasn't myself. But now that she's awake and on the road to recovery, I feel much better." I winked at her and wiggled my pinky at her again. "So, you think you can bend the rules just this one time? I'm pretty sure that wearing this ring will speed up her recovery."

"I think you're right." She walked out from behind the nurses' station, beckoning me to follow her. "Come on with me. I'm going to put this down as a therapist's visit. That means you get an hour with her. This is the kind of therapy she really needs right now too."

I had an in now, and I would be using it to my advantage. "Thank you. You're a saint."

"So I've been told." She took me right to Nina. "She's resting, but feel free to hold her hand. She might wake up for you." She pulled the curtain to cover the majority of the glass wall, giving us a bit of privacy. "I'll come back in an hour to let you know when your time's up."

With a nod, I turned back to look at Nina. The swelling in her head was gone. The bruises had healed, and the cuts were nearly gone too. I ran my fingertips across her cheeks, and her eyes fluttered open. "You," she sighed.

"Yeah, it's me." I leaned over and barely touched my lips to hers. The wave that rushed over me threatened to take me under. But I hung on, staying strong for her. "I've missed you."

Her eyes glistened with tears that began to flow down her face. "I've missed you since I woke up. I wish you could've been here."

"Me too." I took her hand, which had bruises on top of it where the IV went in. Moving my thumb over it carefully, I tried not to break down as I thought about all that she'd gone through.

"The doctor came in a little while ago. He says I've got a long road ahead of me, but it's a road that will lead me back to good health. Apparently, I will live." She laughed a little, then sighed.

I pulled the ring off my pinky and showed it to her. "Apparently, I'll live too. A happy life with you in it for as long as the good Lord allows." I slid the ring back onto her finger, then kissed it. "Just so you know, we're getting married as soon as possible, baby."

A sob came out of her, and she began to cry. "I love you so much. You have no idea how much."

Wrapping my arms around her carefully, I held her, whispering,

"I love you more than you know. We have a bright future ahead of us, baby. It's all smooth sailing from here. We've got each other, and that's all we'll ever need."

Nina and I had found our happily ever after, even though the odds had been against us. We both knew it wasn't always going to be easy, but we'd get through the hard times, together.

The End

Did you like this book? Then you'll LOVE Dirty Little Virgin: A Submissives' Secrets Novel 1

School is in session, and the lessons are rock hard!

She wants to write about the domme and my world.
And I'm supposed to teach her, not take her.
But her feisty manner begs to be tamed.
Her innocence begs to be taken.
I know my whip can bring her into submission.
Her young body begs for my harsh and experienced touch.
I'll train her to accept pain to gain pleasure.
The seclusion is temporary, as is our contract.
But what if I want something more permanent?

I'm not supposed to fall for my subs but I seem to be breaking all my own rules...

Start reading Dirty Little Virgin NOW!

https://books2read.com/u/4jarKo